THE CURIOUS WORLD OF
KATIE HINGE

Best Wishes

THE CURIOUS WORLD OF
KATIE HINGE

by
Colin R. Parsons

Cover Illustration by Derek Jones

The Curious World of Katie Hinge

ISBN 978-0-9570278-0-0

First Published 2011

by

TallyBerry

United Kingdom

Printed by Glenside Printing

Acknowledgements

Special thanks to:

My wife Jan for all the dedication and loyalty she has shown over the years, from the very beginning. Without her pushing me onwards, none of my journey would have been possible. Kristoffer and Ryan, my two sons, for all their support. Mam, who always believed in me and is always there with a helping hand. I love you, Mam. And to Dad, who never saw my work.

Elsie, no longer with us, but believed in everything I did. Derek Jones, a very dear and close friend; he also illustrated the cover of this book and helped me on many of my other projects. His artwork is always wonderfully orchestrated and captivating.

Also, my Auntie Olive for her support.

A special thank you to *you* for reading and enjoying my books

Chapter 1

Almost a Year

It was the eve of World Book Day and that in itself brought on a chill of nerves. Almost a year since it all happened! Katie Hinge had carried on her life in a sort of daze of memories. Her doctor (a psychiatrist), Dr Sheldon, had been helping her throughout, so now it almost seemed like an old, made-up story.

Meeting, befriending and losing Shelley Vendor (her best friend) had never taken place. That is what the good doctor had embedded in her mind. She, Katie, had never entered the world of Reflections where she had not befriended a monkey called Monkey. She'd also never come up against the evil Shadrack Scarrat and his deadly Razzard wolves; it was all a figment of her wild imagination. This is what she was supposed to believe. There was a brooch or jewel embedded in a book that had brought the entire story about. It was the centrepiece of the World Book Day Exhibition. The school trip that Katie had explained to the good Dr Sheldon that she and Shelley had taken. That precious stone that had brought Katie back to the real world, but that wasn't true either and didn't happen, according to Dr Sheldon. Oh, the doctor believed she'd gone on the trip, but that was all. Katie though, through all the brainwashing she'd endured, knew differently.

Katie actually had 'The Stone' in her possession, so she knew she was telling the truth. She hadn't shown it to anyone she didn't trust, and always kept it in a safe place. She definitely didn't show or tell Dr Sheldon that she had it; it was her secret. She didn't tell her parents because they didn't believe her either. They were so distraught about Katie's imaginary friend that they'd introduced the psychiatrist in the first place, which made her very unhappy. But she had confided in one person and one person only: Tina Sprockett. Tina Sprockett was a very private person and never had any friends, but after Katie had allegedly lost her best friend Shelley Vendor, she began to talk to Tina. Tina was glad of the company because she was always getting bullied by the dreaded Scrag Girls, just like Shelley had been. And when 'Mental Katie' came along, so called by the Scrag Girls, they left Tina and Katie alone. The word had spread like wildfire throughout the school that Katie was seeing a 'Shrink.' Katie unnerved the gang with her steely-eyed look and strange stories (that she'd made up to keep them at bay). Tina didn't know whether to believe her or not about her friend Shelley, so they kept a quirky relationship. At times, Katie didn't know whether the adventure was true or not either, because the longer the time passed, the more faded the images became. What *did* keep Katie going, though, was the fact that the school were again running the same trip. She thought as she made her way home from school that day, that maybe, just maybe she could make one more trip to Reflections. Reflections: The strange but mysterious place that she and Shelley had travelled to. It was a wonderfully pretty landscape, but with a very sinister hidden background that included scary creatures that lived there.

That night, Katie went to bed earlier than usual. She lay comfortably snuggled in her duvet and closed her eyes. Images of Shelley, Kevin and Monkey danced around her mind like a montage playing out on an old film reel. They were all laughing together and calling to her to join them – it seemed so real. Seeing Shelley happy again brought a warm smile to her sad face. These days, she didn't smile or laugh much, not like she used to. She hadn't smiled much since she'd got back – since it all fell apart and left her a shell of her former self. And session after session with Dr Sheldon meant the glum expression she wore was almost a permanent fixture.

She must have drifted off into a light sleep, because something roused her and when she came round she felt groggy and listless.

It was precisely two o'clock in the morning when it happened! There was no noise or vibration that pulled her from her dreams. There was a steady pulsing of light though, that throbbed annoyingly in her room. Its blue glow evolved eventually into a vibrant, rich, purple. It felt like a silent alarm clock that wouldn't shut off. Her heavily sleepy eyelids cracked open and she was confronted with a violent assault on her pupils.

'Arrgh...' she shrieked and the sudden noise cut into the dead silence. The brightness made her squint, so she pulled the bed sheet over her face as a barrier. But it was no good, the light throbbed menacingly through the cotton material. Katie eventually tossed it off her face and rolled over onto her left side and peered at the clock through slit eyes. But everything was too distorted to make out. She let out a huge sigh from within and rubbed her tired, droopy lids, but still everything was a blur. She rubbed them again and wiped away crumbs of sleep, then stared intently at the digital display. Slowly it released the luminous, oblong picture of its digits.

'Oow, two o'clock, what's happening?' she slurred, barely having the strength to utter the words. She reached out in a lethargic struggle and tried to turn off the alarm, but, to her utter disillusionment, it wasn't on! 'Aaaargh,' she growled again and through the slits that were now becoming wider, she saw the silhouettes of her slippers appearing and disappearing on the wall! Katie was way too drowsy to register what was going on. So she rolled onto her back and over onto her right side and let out another big puff of breath.

'This is not happening,' she grunted. With all her might she tried to go back off to sleep, but her eyelids acted like cheap roller blinds that let in the relentless bombardment of the pulsing light.

'Ouch,' she grumbled again and flicked her eyes wide open this time. 'What is bloody happening?' she cursed. Once again she rolled onto her left side and by now she was wide awake. There was no going back to sleep in a hurry. The image of her footwear was still doing the flashy thing on the wall. She stared at it for a while, not able to do anything else.

'If it's not my alarm clock, *then what is it?*' She stretched out the last words in annoyance. Curiosity took hold and she twisted her body and leaned over the bed. It was coming from below; yes it was definitely coming from the dark recess under her bed. It reminded her of the Bat-phone from old episodes of 'Batman' that she and her father used to watch. She curled herself over the mattress to the underside of the bed, like a human hook. In a sort of half a handstand and balancing precariously, she peered at the underside of her bed. Then it hit her! The shoe box she'd kept hidden away from the world was now on its side. Mum must have knocked it over when she was vacuuming my room, she surmised. The stone was outside it and flashing away like crazy. Katie was dumbstruck! It hadn't made any sign of life in all the time she'd kept it hidden. Since she'd come back, she'd brought it out on many occasions and tried to get it to do something – she'd shaken it, rubbed it, talked to it and even listened to it, but it hadn't made a sound or any kind of signal. Dormant for a solid year and now it comes to life, what's that all about, she pondered? With all this going on in her head and the blood pumping into her skull from gravity, Katie hadn't got the balance right. Her hips jolted forward with the top-heavy shift in weight and her whole body slid off the bed and tumbled into a forward roll.

'Oh God!' she squeaked and slumped onto her back, landing with a loud thunk! The sound echoed throughout the house and in the deadly quiet of night amplified a hundred times. Katie was now half-winded and unable to move as a last gasp of air left her mouth. She came to her senses when she heard her mother's shuffling footsteps along the landing. She sucked in oxygen in a panic and immediately tried to straighten up but, not realising she'd slid a fraction under the bed, banged her head on the wooden framework.

'Oooww!' she winced, but had no time to nurse her fast-numbing forehead and grappled for her pillow. Once she'd grabbed it, she stuffed it under the bed and put it discreetly in the way of the stone, blocking the flashing light. There was a gentle but urgent tap-tap-tap on Katie's bedroom door. She scrambled into bed and lay as still as a corpse and tried to calm her rapid breathing.

'Are you all right, Katie?' Her mother's concerned, but muffled voice emitted from the other side of the door. Mrs Hinge opened it a crack.

'Yeah Mum, sorry, I fell out of bed,' Katie replied gingerly, almost breathless. 'Sorry to wake you,' she hissed from the darkness. Katie's mother peered into the room, squinting to make out her daughter's shape.

'Are you sure you're all right, dear?' her mother persisted. 'I'm coming in.'

'No Mum, go back to bed – I'm all right, honest,' Katie replied sharply.

'Well, OK dear, if you're sure, night then,' her mother said, still a little confused.

'Night Mum.' Katie heard the door click shut. Her mother's padded footsteps faded as she returned to her own bedroom. Katie let out a gasp, 'Wow, that was close. Ohhhh.' Then she felt the burning pain of her head and placed her hand gently on the thickening skin. There was a lump forming. She made a hissing sound by sucking in air through her teeth. 'Oh, that'll be sore in the morning,'she whispered. 'I'm glad my hair is long, I can hide that with my fringe.' She spoke softly. 'Don't want the good doctor to think I'm self-harming, or that will be another few pages filled up in her book,' she said sarcastically. Once her mum was safely back in her room, Katie immediately slipped off the bed and pulled out the pillow. She took a quick glance back at the bedroom door, but just to make sure it was secure she made her way quietly to it and touched the handle. It was shut! Then she turned back to the stone. She knelt on the floor and leaned onto her belly – there it was, still throbbing away. She reached out with a trembling hand, not knowing what was in store. The brooch was just lying there like a Christmas ornament. It brought all the memories of her adventure flooding back and she savoured it for a minute or so. After reminiscing, she slowly edged her trembling hand towards it again. Before she touched it, she considered if it would be hot or not. So she cautiously dabbed at it, as you would with the hot handle of a bubbling saucepan. It was stone cold to the touch! Mmmm, she thought, so should she pick it up? It looked as if it were begging to be held. She bit her lip in contemplation. Then a strange thing happened when she finally *did* rest her hand on the flashing stone . . . it stopped glowing and the room was left in darkness! Katie was shocked! What had she done wrong? She pulled her hand away sharply, but it didn't make any difference. The stone lay dead.

'Owww, what have I done?' she sulked. A huge sinking feeling engulfed her whole body. 'Is that it, nothing more? A whole year and it glows for a few minutes, damn.' All her hopes and the excitement died with the jewel. She shook her head and closed her eyes for a moment. Was all this happening at all or was it the fact that she missed Shelley and wanted something to happen? Katie quickly snatched the jewel in her left hand and switched on her bedside lamp with her right. The sheer weight of disappointment was overwhelming and showed heavily on her face. She held the stone and gripped its smoothness in her fist. She vigorously shook it to see if it would react, but it didn't. Her face winced as if in pain. She began to quietly sob and grabbed a tissue from a box on her bedside table. Warm tears escaped her eyes and streamed down her cheeks.

'Oh no, no,' she whispered regretfully, 'come back on and prove that I'm not crazy, please,' she pleaded to the stone. 'I must be mad. I've just been fooling myself. Dr Sheldon was right,' she said through moist, tear-streaked lips.

'Don't cry Katie, I can't bear it. You're not mad.' Katie stopped immediately and let out a gasp that sounded like escaping gas. She looked around the room, everything appeared normal. She looked at the stone and shook it. 'What am I doing? Where on earth did the voice come from?' The orange glow of her lamp depicted her wardrobe and mirror and peach curtains, but nothing that resembled anybody else in the room. She was frightened and tensed, which brought short sharp breaths. But although she was frightened, she was curious, too. She somehow recognised the voice.

How was that possible?

'Katie, please don't cry.' The soft voice wafted over her again like an old favourite song.

'Who . . . who's there?' she stuttered nervously. Then it suddenly dawned on her who the voice belonged to. No, it can't be, can it? She shrugged the thought. She was in denial, something Dr Sheldon had planted in her vocabulary. What was happening? Was she hearing things now, too? No wonder they called her Mental Katie, maybe the Scrag Girls were right about her. Maybe she *was* crazy. 'Ah, to hell with it,' she said and called out.

'Monkey . . . Monkey, is that you?' she gushed and immediately realised her parents might hear her. She dropped the high tone to a whisper and creased her face in punishment and winced as if in pain. Did her parents hear her? She held her breath. No they hadn't, she thought, or they would have been here by now. She even used a whisper in her thoughts so as not to wake her parents. Silly, but it seemed crucial.

'Yes, of course it is, who did you think it would be?' Monkey scolded. This brought a wry smile to Katie's face, even a warm feeling inside. It was Monkey; only *he* was that sarcastic, she thought.

'Where are you? I can't see you.' She whispered excitedly in the lowest hushed tone she could muster. 'Come out and show yourself,' she insisted.

'I can't, Katie. Why are you whispering?' He again commented with a touch of annoyance.

'Can't you see me Monkey? It's the middle of the

night and I don't want to wake my parents,' she retorted, and shook her head in disbelief. 'Why can't you see me?' she badgered whilst still clutching the stone.

'I'm not with you as such. I'm in Reflections. My voice is being carried to you somehow.' He bounced back with a slight echo.

'It must be the stone,' she said excitedly. 'It's true, it really is true . . . I'm not mad. I didn't make it all up.' Katie gushed and took a moment to reflect. Ironically, she'd been almost brainwashed by her psychiatrist into believing she'd made it all up. It came as a great relief to finally know that it was all true.

'No, of course you're not mad, who told you that?' he said flippantly.

'My . . . uh . . . doctor.' She stumbled, suddenly feeling awkward and embarrassed about seeing one.

'Doctors, what do they know?' he retorted bitterly. 'I knew you had the stone,' he said, changing the subject immediately. 'Oh, Katie, it's so good to hear your voice.' His manner softened.

'Monkey, I never thought I'd ever hear your voice again either. They tried to make me believe it never happened.' She was almost hyperventilating, her voice lifting as she spoke. It was then she heard her parents' muffled voices through her bedroom wall.

'Does she know what time it is?', her father's voice grumbled, as though coming from inside a box. 'I've got to get up early for work,' his groans becoming more audible.

'Monkey, shh . . . my mother is coming, she must have heard us.' Katie quickly slid back into the bed and flicked off the lamp. She wrapped the sheets around her, closed her eyes and groaned as if dreaming.

'Katie, Katie, are you all right, love?' Her mother called out in a low pitch and she opened the door again. Mrs Hinge stood there listening for a few moments and smiled to herself; she's dreaming, she thought. She then entered the room and sat on the edge of Katie's bed and gently stroked her hair back fondly. She noticed her pillow on the floor. Ah, she's been restless again, she sighed. Katie's head was on her support pillow and her mother left the other on the floor so she wouldn't disturb her.

'Shh, Katie, you're all right – go to sleep,' Katie's mother gently whispered and the mumblings of Katie's bogus sleep drifted away. Mrs Hinge, fulfilled that she'd done her good mothering deed, went back to bed. Katie waited. A pool of sweat welled on her temple and overflowed in a seam down her brow and eventually onto the pillow. It went quiet again and she whispered to her friend.

'Monkey, are you still there?'

'Yes, Katie. Look, I haven't much time,' he replied from somewhere and nowhere in the room.

'We must keep our voices down this time or Mum and Dad will suspect something,' she announced urgently, but as quietly as she could. 'Why have you come to me, Monkey?'

'Don't you want to hear from me?' Monkey replied

sombrely. 'I thought you'd have missed me,' he continued, sounding totally downbeat.

'Of course I do, I've missed you lots and lots. Don't you say that again,' she snapped, feeling tired and angry. 'I've missed everybody, especially Shelley.' There was a pause. 'Monkey, are you still there? Monkey . . . what's happened?'

'Shelley needs your help, Katie,' he said, his voice sweeping through the darkness, more urgently now. 'She's in trouble and may be in terrible danger.' The word 'Shelley' filled Katie with a deep, trembling emotion and another flow of tears streamed from her eyes. She hadn't heard her name in the present tense for a long time.

'What trouble, Monkey? Is she all right? What can I do to help, Monkey?' Katie sobbed. 'What's happened to her? Why does she need my help?' she questioned with concern, her eyes wide, reflected in the mirror of her little room.

'She's been taken,' was the curt reply. 'Kidnapped!'

'By whom?' Katie asked angrily. 'Not by Scarrat. Please, not by him.' She recalled the last time she was in Reflections with Shelley and that Shadrack Scarrat was trying to kill Shelley. But he turned good when he realised she was his daughter.

'No, not Shadrack.' There was a pause. 'Lord Fairbourne and Shadrack are both . . . dead!' There was a silence that can only be described as dead air. Katie's mind was working overtime. She breathed hard, and horrible images in black and red contorted themselves in the darkness. Scary images of monsters, and weird, evolving creatures that only the mind can conjure up on the black canvas of night.

'Dead, but by whom? I thought the Plogs had gone from Reflections,' Katie continued (the Plogs being the creatures under Shadrack Scarrat's command until they tried to overthrow him and were beaten by his father, Lord Fairbourne, never to return).

'No, Katie, there's another threat now, no one knows who or what it is, but it's a silent, dark, evil,' Monkey continued. 'I'm at a loss and, since the Dawn of Reflections is imminent, you must come back and help me find Shelley,' he pleaded. 'It's the only time you can return.'

'But how?' she asked truthfully. 'I'm here and you're there.'

'You must go back to the same place to re-enter Reflections. It's the only way.' He paused again, 'I'll be waiting.' Then Monkey's voice faded into the background.

'But Monkey, where's Kevin, can't he help?' She was filled with questions, but Monkey didn't reply. 'Monkey . . . Monkey.' She tried to call out with a hiss, but there was still no answer. Almost breathlessly, she sat there fully awake and terribly shocked. She quietly called twice more to no avail. She glanced down at the clock once more. It read two twenty-one. Her mind was awash with all kinds of theories and frightening thoughts. Shadrack and Lord Fairbourne dead! I must get some sleep, she thought. If I'm to help find Shelley,

I need to go to sleep. She grabbed the stone and put it on her cabinet and lay in the darkness. Pictures formed in front of her like a cinema screen. Not happy pictures now though, but scary and deadly images; images of horrible, wolven faces and sharp teeth, so vivid it felt as if she was already back in Reflections. She shook her head vigorously. 'I must go to sleep.' She repeated the words as if giving herself instructions. Her mind was way too full to let her escape to slumber, but eventually it did.

Chapter 2

Lost

Katie sat at the table that morning, spooning her breakfast into her mouth in a stupor. Her night of disturbed sleep was already taking its toll in the shape of droopy eyelids and a lacklustre refrain. She rested her left elbow on the table and propped up her head as she scooped up the last couple of spoonfuls. He mind was still swimming from the strange night of voices in the darkness. She was so enthralled by it all that she didn't hear her mother's voice raking in the background.

'Katie . . . Katie. Are you sure you'll be all right to go to school today, Katie?' her mother asked, whilst resting a sympathetic hand on Katie's shoulder and feeling a little worried about her. 'You'll be a long way from home.' Mrs Hinge said, remembering the school trip. Katie looked up from her cereal bowl and smiled a tired smile, which she could barely bring to her mouth.

'Mum, I'll be fine, honestly. Once I've come around a bit, I'll be back to my happy, clappy self. Look, watch; I'm smiling and getting ready,' she said and finished up her meal and began busily preparing for school.

'If only that were true, Kate. I would love to see you smile a real happy smile again; I've missed that *so* much.' She stood gazing at her little girl. 'Just enjoy yourself today and I'll have your favourite for tea when you get home,' her mother said and kissed her on the forehead before adding, 'but if you're feeling unwell, just get the teacher to ring me. I'll sort something out to get you home, don't you worry.'

'Thanks Mum, I know you will,' Katie answered, still forcing the last of a smile. Katie soon perked up for real when she realised what adventure she had to relay to Tina when she got to school. She bolted up to her room before she left, to pick up the precious stone. It was still in its dormant state and she felt a little sad looking at it, but made sure that it was placed safely in her pocket. She patted, affectionately, the small lump it made in her trousers. She made her way to school, deep in thought, ignoring everything around her. Was it really a year since she'd lost her best friend? She questioned herself. Once at school, the teachers went through the same routine as the previous year. Still preoccupied, she boarded the bus with Tina Sprockett and was once again heading to the same event and sitting in the same seats. It was also ironic that they had the same teachers that she and Shelley had travelled with the last time. Mrs Gillies, still as overbearing as ever, was in charge. Her downtrodden understudy Mrs Downs (previously Miss Shanks or 'Shanksy') was trapped on the inside of the seat with the Deputy Head. A deep pang of loss filled the pit of Katie's stomach as Mr Jones revved the old engine and the vehicle shuddered into action. Shelley, I miss you so much; the thought stabbed at her like a sharp dagger. She almost felt like crying.

'What did you want to tell me?' Tina asked excitedly, her eyes glimmering with anticipation, and Katie explained every detail.

'So, she really does exist then, you're sure?' she said as Katie finished the story. This prompted Tina with the question, 'but why can't I and everyone else re-member her, then?' She stared at Katie, finding it hard to believe her.

'I don't know, Tina, but I will find a way to prove it to you one day, I promise,' she concluded, and then sat back and was left to her thoughts. This time around, the bus trip seemed to take a lot longer than the last time. Houses swept by and they were soon ploughing down the motorway. Katie had always hated any jour-ney to a destination, but enjoyed the experience of being there and eventually coming home. This time, though, she had real doubts.

The bus finally neared its destination and Katie pressed her face against the window. The sight of the building sent a shiver through her body. It was a year ago, but it seemed, as they entered the bus park, to have only just happened! She swallowed hard and stepped off the platform onto the dusty gravel pathway. She took a few deep breaths and closed her eyes, all the time willing a way in which she could return and again meet her best friend.

'Are you all right, Katie?' The timid, melodic tone of Mrs Downs streamed into her ear. Katie turned to her and smiled a broad, contented smile. 'You look sad.'

'I'm fine, Mrs Downs, please don't worry.' Katie re-sponded, still feeling a bit awkward at calling her Mrs instead of Miss – and especially Downs instead of Shanks. The last time she was here, the young teacher had taken her to a nurse before they'd left for home. Katie had bumped her head and this brought back a worrying memory for Mrs Downs. Mrs Gillies took roll call and when she was satisfied everything was proper, she led the way in. Familiarity washed over Katie in the shape of the foyer and counter. This was where Shelley was almost blamed for a display toppling over, but it was, in fact, a malicious act by the Scrag Girls. There was also the warmth of enjoyment as she saw the pictures of famous authors adorning the walls on the way through. It had only just occurred to her that they had missed the very author they wanted to meet the last time. Katie remembered that she stood in the queue, and just before she'd had time to meet Niloc Snosrap, she'd had to go and help Shelley. And that's where their adventure began. Katie was instantly drawn to the spot where it had all taken place. Tina eased back and let Katie plough forward; a sense of anticipation gave her the worried look on her face.

'What's the matter, Tina, aren't you coming?' Katie asked, when she'd noticed her friend was no longer with her. Tina froze to the spot.

'I...I'll wait here, Katie,' she stammered, with a sense of foreboding, biting her bottom lip nervously.

'But the doorway is just over there,' Katie expressed annoyingly and pointed in the desired direction. At the sight of the door, Tina took a step backwards.

'No, I'm fine; I'll wa-it for you to co-me back,' she stumbled. Katie could see that she was scared, so scared in fact that she began twisting and slowly strangling the strap of her handbag.

'Oh, all right then, I'll see you later,' she snapped and gave Tina a look that could have frozen custard. She puffed in annoyance and clenched her teeth tight shut. But her refrain soon turned from anger to excitement. There was the sudden feel of warmth in her pocket, the warmth of life returning to the stone. The diamond again began pulsing, as it had in the early hours of that morning. This new lease of life spurred her on, gave her hope. Retracing her steps, she made her way to the familiar door marked 'Staff only' (the very same door that they'd entered previously, and on the other side had taken them to Reflections). Her insides felt as though a million butterflies were taking off in unison. With a strange, twitchy excitement, she edged towards it and glanced from side to side to make sure no one was watching. With one last deep breath she walked through! Once inside, she was swallowed up in the semi-darkness of the corridor. The only source of light was coming from amber orbs, intermittently fixed along the wall (it was all coming back to her now). She fumbled inside her pocket and drew out the gem. Its magnificence reflected her face into bleached blue porcelain and brought an angelic substance to the passageway. Its beam also caught the rim of a perfectly-rounded circle of white light that was suspended in mid-air. She gasped! Her mouth was biscuit dry, the pounding inside her chest vibrated her skin and her breathing was short and wavering. This was it! This is what she'd been waiting for, for the past year – to escape from Dr Sheldon and the Scrag Girls and everyone else who thought her a weirdo.

'Oh, my god,' she whispered, at last realising that she was only a step away from another world. She cautiously moved towards the ring and very nervously reached out with her left hand, the stone firmly fixed in her right. Her splayed fingers, upon touching the surface inside the ring, dissolved into the black. This left weird-looking, ugly finger stumps that made her feel sick. She retracted immediately, even retching at the sight of their deformity, but realising they were whole again when removed. She tried to swallow saliva and winced at the bitter, acid taste of vomit that had surfaced and retracted. Katie quickly pushed that memory to one side and curiously felt around the outer side of the circle. It wasn't hot to the touch like she'd expected it to be. She curled her arm around the back, again losing her limb in the process, but this time not troubled by it. It was there and wasn't there, most peculiar, she thought, and began to relax. She pulled her arm from around the back and again probed the black surface of the ring with her hand. There was a definite surge of energy gently sucking on her fingertips. She again whipped it away anxiously, her heart beating hard enough to power a small aircraft. Her pulse was racing and her hands were clammy; a thin layer of sweat appeared on her upper lip.

'What am I doing? What if I can't come back? What if no one remembers me if I do return? Oh, Shelley.' The picture of Shelley in her mind gave her the power to continue.

'Oh, what the hell,' she said as, finally, she had made up her mind. Nothing was going to stop her now. She'd weighed up the idea of staying behind in her miserable existence, or the desperate need to help her friend. On the third attempt, she pushed even further into the abyss. Fingers, hand, forearm up to the elbow and even a little further. She groped inside as if trying to feel for something, but she didn't know what. She somehow expected it to feel sticky and warm, like heated treacle. It was neither.

'Whoooaaa,' she wailed in panic. This time the enigma, the unknown force, wouldn't let go and gripped her arm solidly!

'Arrrgh, let go, let go,' she heard herself saying. The glossy black liquid began to suck her in like sinking sand. Katie tried to scream, but only let out a whimper as she frantically tried to pull back. She *did* scream in her mind and tugged with all her might, but it didn't matter how hard she pulled, she couldn't release it. She knew she couldn't resist forever, but wanted to enter Reflections on her own terms. But the overpowering suction had pulled her up to her shoulder. The magnetic force was relentless and the harder she resisted the more it drained her energy.

'I can't do this, I-I can't.' She was shaking now and breathing at a rapid rate. She raised her left arm and, whilst still gripping the stone, tried to stop herself by grasping the edge of the circle. But there was nothing to hold on to and her left arm was swallowed up too! The immense pressure pulled at the rest of her body like a giant vacuum cleaner and she was the dirt.

It was at this point that Tina, filled with fright and curiosity, burst in through the door, only to see her friend's feet disappearing into the suspended hole in the air. It was then that she lunged after Katie and tried to grab her feet, but she was too late! Once her body had been pulled off the ground and into the black, the whole apparition dissolved. Tina fell backwards to the ground. She got straight up, standing bewildered. Tears filled her eyes and ran down her face.

'Katie, Katie!' Tina screamed, but Katie, the stone and the circle were gone! Tina was left sitting in the darkened passage wondering what to tell her teachers.

'I must find Mrs Downs,' she said in panic. She got

up and ran through the door into the noisy hall. She was filled with fear for her friend and the fear of trying to explain to Mrs Downs what had just happened. Tina threaded her way through the advancing excited crowds of autograph hunters. Perspiration seeped on to her forehead and a hot, itchy feeling prickled her scalp. People looked on in bewilderment and anger at her persistent pushing. Where is she? Where is she? Tina's mind was swirling. She stopped dead in her tracks when she caught sight of Mrs Gillies, the only person she didn't want to see. Mrs Gillies seemed to be in an agitated state. She stood with her feet tapping the floor and an impatient look on her face.

Where are you, Mrs Downs? Tina questioned in her mind. She can't be far from Mrs Gillies she thought again. Even if Mrs Downs wanted to be somewhere else, Gillies would eventually find her. Ah, there she was and it all fell into place. Gillies had to wait for Mrs Downs to have her book signed. The queue was long and Mrs Downs was only halfway and that meant that Mrs Gillies had been waiting a while already . . . good! Maybe she would get really bored and move on to somewhere else so that she could get the younger teacher on her own. Tina didn't want to explain anything in front of Mrs Gillies yet! There would be lots of questions from Mrs Downs first and then they could involve the Head. Still in a state of dread, Tina hid in the constant flowing crowd and melted away behind the safety of a pillar. What was she going to say? Katie fell into a magical hole and now she's gone! How would that sound? The longer she waited, the calmer she became. Katie said this would happen and nobody believed her, not even me at first, Tina thought. Still, she was sceptical at the idea of her friend slipping off to Reflections. Has she actually gone there? Tina was in total disarray. With all the thoughts in her head bouncing around, she hadn't noticed Mrs Gillies drifting off. Mrs Downs was almost at the end of the queue. She waited for the author to finish signing her book and then she confronted her.

'Mrs Downs,' she said urgently.

'Oh, Tina, everything all right?' Mrs Downs asked matter of factly. 'Have you found your favourite author yet?' An excited smile filled her small, smooth face.

'Uh, no, not yet Miss.' Tina answered.

'Is there something you wanted to ask me?' Mrs Downs waited expectantly and smiled. Her eyes were bright and blue and filled with curiosity.

'Um, well, my friend...'

'Oh good, you've found someone,' the teacher cut in. 'That's great news, Tina – is she from our school?'

'Found someone, Miss?' Tina replied with a quirky look on her face.

'Yes, I noticed you came on your own today. I hoped that you would find someone at this event to spend the day with, and sit by, on the way home,' Mrs Downs said sympathetically. 'But you don't have to worry,' she continued, 'if you can't find anyone, you can spend the day with me and . . . ' There was a pause. 'Mrs Gillies!' she concluded. That knocked Tina off balance. But what about Katie, doesn't she realise that she's missing? Tina thought.

'But Miss, Katie Hinge...'

'Ah, good, you have found a friend, Katie Hinge. That's a strange name. She's obviously not from our school or I would have remembered a name like that.' Mrs Downs smirked. 'As long as you are all right, that's the main thing.' The weight of worrying less about a pupil seemed to lift the pressure. 'Enjoy the rest of the day and I'll see you by the bus.' She looked up from Tina and the smile that she'd carried soon turned sour. She closed her eyes and took a deep breath.

'Yes, she's from another school,' Tina lied.

'Oh . . . there's Mrs Gillies waving to me, I'd better go.' She rolled her eyes up in her head, the look of dread easily masking the warmth of her features. 'Don't be late for the bus, Tina, 3.30pm we're all meeting in the coach park.' A look of sheer misery filled her and off she went, leaving a very confused Tina Sprockett standing alone. This was more than Tina could take. All this time she didn't believe her friend about anything she'd said, but Katie was right all along. Everything she'd told her was true. There really *is* a Shelley Vendor. Now Shelley and Katie are not remembered in this world.

'But I can remember Katie and that will make me sound crazy, if I tell anyone,' she said as the swirl of people danced around her. I don't want to end up with a Dr Sheldon visiting me like she did Katie. The thought of being interrogated by a psychiatrist made her shudder. There's really nothing I can do until Katie comes back – if she comes back! Another icy chill shot through her and she shivered all through her body. Katie, please come back, I'm sorry, you were right all along. I'm sorry I didn't believe you – I feel terrible about not believing you. Tears filled her eyes and a terrible sense of loss welled up inside. She'd just realised that *if* Katie didn't come back, then things would go back to the way they were. Alone in school classes, lunches and the walk home from the bus. She groaned.

Suddenly, she felt a sharp pain in her back and the reality of it all dawned. They were here, like a bad headache that wouldn't go away.

'Move, Sprockett, or die.' The Scrag Girls pushed passed, but Tina eased out of their way. Out of desperation more than anything, Tina went back to the door and walked inside in the hope of finding her friend waiting there.

'Hey, what are you doing here?' A suited security guard walked in behind her.

'I-I was looking for the toilet,' she replied with a tremble.

'Well, you're in the wrong place – this place is out of bounds to the public. You need to go here,' he said, and pointed to a signpost that had 'TOILETS' in big, bold writing written on it.

'Oh, OK, sorry,' she said, and made her way there under the watchful eye of the guard. She stepped inside and walked to the washbasin, twisted the cold water tap and splashed some water on her face. This was to try and wash away the events that had taken place in the last half-hour. But in reality it didn't change anything. Katie was gone and Tina would just have to forget about her. She dried her face on a paper towel and walked out of the door, back into the hall.

Chapter 3

Reacquainted

The sensation of being pulled by an unknown force was overwhelming and at first she could barely breathe. The sensation of falling in complete darkness was unnerving to say the least. Was she upside down, sideways or upright? She couldn't tell.

She felt quite sick. It was like falling from a great height through a crack in the earth. Dizzy and disorientated, she was all those things, and all she wanted was for it to stop. The only thing she could hear was the rush of air gushing past her ears, blocking out any other sound. The only thing she could feel was the blast of cold air on her face, arms and legs. She began to panic and desperately tried to cling onto something, anything, but nothing came to hand! Where the hell was she? It didn't take this long the first time around. The first trip to Reflections, she just fell one minute and the next she was there. This was different, this was scary! She wanted to scream and let the world know where she was, but only a strangled whimper escaped her mouth. 'Oh, help me, please, someone come and help me, please,' she gurgled as she spun and tumbled into nothingness. She clenched her eyes tight shut and tensed. She was ready – ready for the inevitable crash landing that would probably result in her instantaneous . . . *Death!*

The constant tumbling around had made her really dizzy, and the bitter hot acidic taste of vomit filled her throat. She tried to keep it down, but it was slowly rising; she retched and swallowed it back hard. She began crying hysterically and tried to cover her ears to stop the constant hiss that filled her head – it was driving her mad.

'Oh, please let it end, let it end. I can't take this any more, please let it sto . . .' She was cut short as a moment or two later she burst out into the open air. By the time she opened her eyes, she had hit a wall of water. SPLASH!

The cold hit her first; then the heavy, leaded water wrapped around her like a weighted cardigan and forcefully pulled her down. Katie was so disorientated that she opened her eyes to focus on where she was. She was met by a bleached wall of white water and millions of escaping bubbles. Again she started to hyperventilate, but then suddenly stopped the struggle. The next moment she relaxed; her instincts for survival took hold and she righted herself. Not knowing how deep she had descended, she began to swim. The air in her lungs pushed her upwards and now she knew in which direction to go. The intense thought of survival spurred her on. She didn't have time to prepare and needed air urgently. With tired limbs, she pushed huge armfuls of water aside and felt the flow helping rather than hindering. She'd always been a good swimmer at school and her slim build acted as a torpedo. Up further and further she went with the rhythm of underwater flight. She could barely hold her breath any more and didn't think she could make it. Sooner than she expected, though, she broke through the surface and finally – air! She gulped for oxygen hungrily as a baby sucks on a bottle of milk. The moment it hit her lungs, it made her cough and choke and she knew she had to get out of there. Unaware of her location, she instinctively began treading water, which made her relax and breathe more steadily again. This was the natural course of survival that she'd learned and had done many a time in her local swimming pool. Now, though totally drained of energy and still disorientated, she frantically searched for land. Through blurred tired eyes she made out a bank and slowly floated toward it.

'Take it steady, girl, you know you can do this. You've done it a million times before, but this is for real.' she told herself. Hope came sooner than later when she felt soft, squishy mud in her hands and a broad grin filled her face. 'Oh, thank God,' she felt herself saying and scrambled forward. With a new zest for life, she clawed her way up through the sludge until her fingertips grasped drier ground and clumps of grass. A stab of excitement urged her on. Finally, she was almost out, almost safe. Only when her toes squelched in caking mud, and then finally dry grass, did she feel relief. It was all too much – the fall, the struggle in the water – and, ultimately, she collapsed into unconsciousness!

***

Her mum poured her a steaming cup of tea with a plateful of custard creams. Oh, the feeling was dreamy and she slunk back into her warm, soft sofa.

'Would you like some more tea, dear?' her Mum asked with a tender smile.

'Ah, yes please, Mum,' Katie answered dreamily.

'Come on Katie, wake up, please wake up.' She blinked her eyes and at first a dark figure stood before her, lingering over her like a large cloud.

'M-u-m,' the word slowly tumbled from her mouth

in a lacklustre effort. When her eyes finally focused, a warm smile curled her parched lips and in a hoarse voice she uttered:

'Mon-key, oh Monkey, it's really you.' She sighed in between shallow breaths, but a definite spark of warmth filled her entire body. She rolled ever so gently onto her back; the weakness of the struggle had taken its toll.

'Arrgh,' she complained.

'Easy now, Katie, take your time.' Monkey's soothing voice caressed her like a child's comfort blanket.

'Oh, Monkey,' she said sleepily and closed her eyes for a few moments. It was bliss shutting her eyes; it felt as though she never wanted to open them again.

'Katie, stay awake, don't sleep,' he insisted and shook her gently to rouse her.

'Oh . . . where am I?' she asked, as she became more coherent. Through slitted eyes, she scanned the landscape whilst easing herself up onto her elbows. Her body felt like a ton weight and she winced as she shifted. It was a great effort to even blink her eyes.

'You don't know?' he remarked ominously. She stared into his black, hypnotic eyes and giggled – and even that hurt her chest.

'Oh, it's so good to see you, Monkey. It's been way too long,' she added and reasserted herself. 'Now hold on a minute and let me have a little time to recover. You haven't changed one little bit,' she said with fondness. Soon her surroundings became clearer and unfolded like a great big picture book. She was lying by the side of a river that cut jaggedly right through the landscape. It was beautiful and very familiar. Also resting on the surface of the river, overwhelming, but not dipping into it was the bridge. Yes, 'the bridge', she remembered with a gush of excitement. 'Settlers Bridge,' she cast her mind back. It was the only bridge she knew that floated in mid air; strange very strange. But everything was different in Reflections. This was the norm in a strange and sometimes magical world.

'Hello, old friend' she beamed, then it dawned on her like a rush of blood to the head . . . Shelley!

'Monkey, where's Shelley, what's happened?', she probed all in one huge breath, and sat up fully. Her head swam and images floated past until she steadied herself.

'It's a long story and I'll tell you everything once you've had some food – you must be hungry,' he surmised. Ah, food; she hadn't thought of that with all the excitement, but her stomach soon reminded her that she hadn't eaten for a while. But she *did* feel calmer now, especially as the golden summer sun beamed down onto her back, making her sodden clothes steam. It also dawned on her that it was March here, and spring in her own world – but in Reflections, March was the middle of summer. And Katie loved everything about the summer. She shivered just casting her mind back to the cold harsh winter she'd dragged herself through, a winter that didn't seem to want to end. But now the sun lashed down on a lush, brightly-coloured landscape that made you want to stay there and not move a muscle.

'Katie, are you all right?' Monkey's voice came spilling into her thoughts.

'Yeah, yes sorry Monkey, what were you saying? Oh yeah, food; come on then, lead me to it.' She felt a new sense of purpose after a year-long battle with her psychiatrist. It was all true, everything, and had been all along. She had tried to tell her mother at first, but that's when her parents had got frightened and brought in Dr Sheldon. They didn't understand. It wasn't really their fault. It was a crazy story if anyone thought about it. She snapped back to the present.

'Monkey, the Plogs aren't back, are they?' she asked, thinking this was the reason for her being here.

'No Katie,' Monkey replied with a long puff – just thinking of those horrible creatures was enough to make him sweat. 'They have long gone. Come on, up you get, it's not far to my new home,' he spoke with pride. Katie clambered onto her jellified legs and took a few wobbly steps. She'd forgotten how draining swimming was, especially as she hadn't done it for a while and had been tumble-dried in the process.

'You sure you're all right to walk?' Monkey asked with concern.

'Just let me take a few more steps and I'll be fine, honestly' she said abruptly, and gave him a cheeky grin. He just shook his head; he remembered how stubborn she could be. Monkey led the way with his unsteady friend in tow. They walked for a little while, up a small incline and into the outer edges of a forest. They continued on into the comfortable warmth of the day, with the shading of oak trees towering above. Katie basked in the pleasant indulgence of a short burst of a breeze. Another smile engulfed her small, oval face; this is wonderful, she thought. It felt good to get away from her normal life. After some time, she turned to her friend.

'How much further, Monkey?' she asked, feeling tired after her ordeal.

'We're here,' he announced with a certain amount of glee.

'Where exactly; I can't see anything but the forest?' She scrutinised the area, craning her neck from side to side. They were standing on the inner crest of a wooded glade with no sign of any type of hut or encampment. 'Are you sure?' she asked, thinking he didn't know his own home.

'Here, look.' Monkey had already moved towards a mound of grass tucked to one side of a broad oak tree. If Katie hadn't been shown, she would never have seen it. On closer inspection though, Monkey showed her an entrance that was hidden by overhanging foliage.

'What is it, a hole?' she asked with a dash of sarcasm.

'No,' he stared deep into her eyes and could tell she was teasing him. 'Come on.' He walked inside and promptly disappeared. Katie stooped down on all fours and eased on inside behind him, in a very unladylike fashion. With trepidation, she followed him, but only to find a large hole for an entrance and a short tunnel beyond. It was black, pitch black, and reminded her of the dark journey she'd just taken. And she was understandably concerned but put her trust fully in Monkey. The tunnel sloped into a much larger cavern and once inside found she could fully stand up. Monkey had already lit two candles which brought the home to life in a yellow glow. It was cool inside and damp, but with some crude furniture, such as a bench and table upon which one of the candles was burning. Also, there was a bed to the left and on the other side of the room an area for cooking. This had a section of criss-crossed logs waiting to be used. Above the logs, suspended by a metal apparatus, was a large pot and above that was a domed piece of metal with sections of pipes which disappeared into the wall and signified a chimney. Light from a second candle, which was perched on a ledge, left a huge shadow of Monkey's back on the wall as he stooped to light the fire.

'Wow, how on earth did you find this place?' she asked curiously. He chuckled and lit dried moss with the same match he'd used for the candles. He winced and blew out the flame just as it burned his fingers. The logs caught and soon there was a spluttering, sparking, fire emerging. The wafting smoke was soon sucked away and escaped through the pipe system.

'It must have been where one of the families lived when they escaped Scarrat Town. You know when the Plogs invaded. Take a seat Katie and I'll make you a nice cup of tea.' He gestured towards the bench.

'This is nice, Monkey, but I much preferred your old place.' she said, reminiscing about the hideaway he once had in a railway carriage.

'I know what you mean, I miss it too. It had every-thing I needed until, as you know, it smashed into a million pieces.' He chuckled as he pondered for a moment and set about making tea. Katie remembered clearly the train carriage rolling freely along the track after being loosened from its moorings. It eventually crashed into a barrier after Katie and Monkey jumped off. The memory lingered, but she soon snapped back to the present. By now her clothes were nearly dry and she sat content on the makeshift furniture in the hovel.

'What's the matter, Katie, you look troubled?' He spoke with a hint of regret.

'It's this place Monkey, Reflections; it's the same place I remember from a year ago, but different somehow,' she replied solemnly.

'I've felt the same for a long time now,' he answered in despair, 'I can't put my finger on it either, but its evil, isn't it?' He said this with a shiver, as the light reflected in his blackened, glassy, eyes.

'So what's this all about then? Shelley mysteriously disappeared and Shadrack and poor Lord Fairbourne dead!' She emphasized on Lord Fairbourne's death because she had taken a dislike to Shadrack Scarrat with their first encounter.

'That's just it Katie, Lord Fairbourne and Shadrack were found dead in their beds and the same night Shelley disappeared,

'What about the people of the town, are they still there? Are they even looking for her?' She added with shrugged shoulders.

'They are still in the town and very scared. They haven't left their homes, except in groups to get food and water. No one is doing anything to find Shelley or find the cause of the problem.' There was a finality in his voice that Katie had never heard before. 'This is why I called you. I knew if Shelley was in trouble you would come running. And here you are.' He offered her a steaming cup of tea as he said it.

'I would have come if *any* of you were in trouble, Monkey,' she said and took a sip. It was wonderful.

She couldn't drink too much in one go, but the hot, soothing, liquid lubricated the back of her dried-out throat and she swallowed. She savoured this for a moment and took another heavy sip; it was heaven. She felt invigorated and continued the conversation with a new strength.

'So where do we start?' she asked with purpose.

'I was hoping you would tell me,' he answered honestly. 'I don't really know where to start either. You were always so good at finding the beginning of something. Remember – I always followed your lead.' He grinned.

'Come on Monkey; are there any clues, anything?' She probed with enthusiasm, sounding like a detective. 'Anything at all?' She looked deep into his eyes, probing for an answer. 'A trail or a witness?'

'Well nothing, really. Whoever did this was quiet and didn't leave any witnesses or clues.' He looked at her blankly, ominously shaking his head.

'So you're telling me the two people who run the town are dead, and Shelley, who is part of the family and royalty, is gone!'

'There's no two ways about it. It was calculated and skilfully done.' Monkey interrupted abruptly.

'But why didn't they ki . . .' Katie stopped, she realised what her next suggestion was going to be and swallowed hard.

'I know what you were going to say, Katie, and I don't understand the logic of this either.' He took a moment and then said, 'I'm glad she's been kidnapped in a way; at least, this evil person or persons wants to keep her alive. She would have been dead like the others otherwise.'

'But what could she possibly have that they want?' She screwed up her forehead in thought. 'I don't understand.'

'We've got to find her and find out,' he said with conviction.

'Monkey.' A thought occurred to her.

'Yes, Katie,' he answered with trepidation.

'Where's Kevin?' She suddenly remembered about the closeness of Shelley and Kevin when she'd last seen them. 'Kevin helped her escape Shadrack Scarrat when they first found Reflections, didn't he? He was a good friend to her,' she said.

'Oh, he's gone in search of her since yesterday.' Monkey looked beyond Katie's shoulder and peered at the dirt wall and continued. 'He was very upset and I'm worried for his safety too!'

'None of this makes any sense.' Katie was dredging the depths of her mind to find an answer, any answer! Then her refrain changed, as if what she'd been looking for suddenly appeared right there in front of her nose.

'What is it, Katie? I know that look.' Monkey mused excitedly.

'Maybe it's the stone. Maybe this evil has the same agenda as the Plogs,' she surmised.

'Perhaps you're right, Katie. I knew you'd find something to go on. Perhaps whoever it is thinks Shelley has or knows where the stone is.' Monkey screwed up his leathery nose. 'That's got to be it.' Katie's face suddenly drained of colour as if she'd been kicked in the stomach.

'The stone!' she shrieked. 'The stone.'

'Yep, I've got it Katie, the stone.' Monkey pursed his lips and scratched his chin.

'But what about it? You've got it, haven't you. You must have to leave Reflections and return.' He repeated blankly. Katie frantically stuffed her hands in her trouser pockets . . . it wasn't there!

'Katie, you all right? You've gone pale again,' Monkey asked concerned.

'The stone, it-it's gone!' she stuttered and then stared into open space, trying to figure out the last time she'd had it. She retraced her journey in her mind, like a picture.

'What do you mean gone? But where?' Monkey reiterated. 'You haven't lost it I hope.'

'Well, I had it in my hand when I left my world and . . .'

'And-and what?' Monkey was getting agitated.

'I can't remember after I hit the water.' She had a look of sheer horror on her smooth face.

'What are you saying?'

'It must be in the . . . river.' There was a pause from the both of them, both knowing there was no way they'd be able to find it now, not if it was at the bottom of the river.

'Oh, my good grief,' was all that Monkey could utter.

'All the time we've been sitting here, it's been lost.' She burst into tears and Monkey immediately put his hairy arm around her, and placed his leathered hand on her shoulder for comfort.

'What are we going to do, Monkey?' She sobbed un-controllably, 'I can't help Shelley without the stone.'

'There, there, Katie – we'll figure a way. We always do.' But this time, in his own mind, he knew it was hopeless.

'We have to find it, Monkey.' Katie raised her head with a new determination. 'We have to at least look for it – Shelley needs our help and we have to find it for her safety.'

'You're right, Katie. Hold on – come to think of it, there's a boat tied to the other side of the bank. It's still light and you never know – if the water's calm enough and clear enough we may, just may, find it.' His heart leapt with a renewed vigour. 'Come on.'

Chapter 4

The Search

It was twilight when they reached the banking, making the surroundings look even more idyllic. The soft, pastel shades of the blue/grey sky framed the scene like a lavishly set painting. The overbearing charm and stature of the bridge stood tall and firm, guarding its beloved river. The river now sent shivers down Katie's spine for two reasons; the first, of course, was her near-death experience of almost drowning. The second was her stupidity for losing the stone somewhere in it. It hurt her that she was wasting time when she should be hot on the trail of her friend, but first things first. The stone had to be found, and quickly. The boat Monkey had mentioned was lazily bobbing on the calm river edge, hitched to the shore by a short peg and a length of rope.

'Who does this boat belong to, Monkey?' Katie asked.

'It must be one of the villagers, I suppose. They won't be coming back in a hurry to use it. Not when there's a killer on the loose,' he said, eyes bulging.

'Oh, Monkey; how could I have been so stupid?' She cried in despair as they approached the old, weather-beaten, fishing boat.

'Katie, stop beating yourself up over this; we'll find it, believe me; somehow we will find it. Now, come on, snap out of it.' Monkey was in no mood for mollycoddling.

'It's no use Monkey, it's obviously too dark now,

isn't it? We'll never find it in this light,' she bleated, staring unconvincingly at the smooth, blackened surface of the water. 'We may as well wait until morning, Monkey, it'll be easier to see then.'

'There's no time to waste Katie, don't you understand? We can't wait until morning! If we do, then we'll be that much further behind,' he barked angrily. 'Look, let's get in the boat and give it a try.' He snapped at her as he gingerly clambered aboard the unsteady vessel. He was worried about Shelley, scared at what may happen to her. And, also, Monkey didn't like boats. He preferred the dry, solid feel of land beneath his feet. He was made to climb trees and roam through dense forests, not clamber into unsteady vessels. 'Untie the rope and get in, Katie.' He snapped again whilst he gripped both sides of the boat, steadying himself as best as he could, his knuckles whitening through his thick, black skin. There was a look of total terror residing on his small face.

'All right, keep your hair on,' Katie retorted as she lifted the loop over the peg and threw it into the boat, accidentally clubbing her furry friend on the back of the head.

'Oi, *Katie*,' he shrieked, and held rigid, fully wanting to rub his head better, but at the same time not wanting to let go, not for anything.

'Oops, sorry, Monkey. I didn't see you in this light.' A little smirk quickly whipped across her face and disappeared when she faced him. She could see that he wasn't going to be the best passenger anyone could have had. She climbed in as steadily as was possible and sat facing him. The boat rocked from side to side and sheer terror filled the chimp's eyes. The crease-marks on his brow and around his eyes multiplied abruptly.

'Katie, take it easy. I don't like this – I don't like it at all,' the frayed voice of Monkey squeaked.

'I didn't realise you don't like boats,' she peered. 'But saying that, I've never actually been in a boat with you before, have I? Don't look so worried, I'm sure I can steer this thing,' she said, peering at the two sun-dried oars laid out in a V-shape either side of her. In her mind, Katie was freaking out; how on earth do I go about this? she pondered, nervously trying not to appear totally out of her depth. She looked at Monkey and gave an unconvincing smile.

'Just keep it steady, please,' he urged, as his knuckles turned even whiter. Katie couldn't help but smirk again and he saw it this time.

'It's not funny, girl, so take that grin off your face now!' he muttered through clenched teeth. She settled herself down as comfortably as she could.

'Are we all set then?' she said, stalling for time. I can do this; I can do this, she repeated in her head. Monkey nodded nervously. There was a slight breeze that wafted across the river, cooling the rocks that held the day's heat. The water gently rippled under its soothing breath. Perched overhead was a big full moon that was uninterrupted by clouds and gently sailed across the open sky. She picked up the oars one by one and slotted each of them in the metal rests provided. She dipped the paddles awkwardly into the river and set about the task of pulling hard at both of them. From the moment she pulled back, they slipped easily out of the water and she fell back with a jolt and banged

her head. Monkey screamed as the boat jerked un-
easily and almost capsized. Fortunately, one oar slid
through its coupling back into the boat, but the other
slipped out into the river.

'Katie, what are you doing?' Monkey was totally
freaking out now.

'Keep your hair on, you stupid chimpanzee,' she
rasped, rubbing her fast-burning scalp. 'Oh, that hurt.'
She winced, and hissed at the pain.

'Quickly Katie, look – the oar, it's floating away,' he
screeched urgently. She hoisted herself back on to the
small plank of wood that acted as her seat, and reached
out into the water. The boat listed to one side and
Monkey gripped on for all he was worth. His eyes were
as big as saucers and he gritted his teeth and screwed
up his face. Katie stretched out and managed to get the
tip of her index finger on to the end of the oar before it
escaped. She walked her fingers over its surface and
slowly brought it back to her. She then lifted it up and
placed it back inside the boat again. She looked
straight into her friend's face, only to find him sitting
as rigid as a statue. She burst out laughing; he looked
like one of those musical monkeys you found in toy
shops that switched on and bashed two cymbals together.

'What are you laughing at?' he snarled, but that, too,
didn't help and sent Katie into deeper fits of laughter.
It seemed that all the tension and depression over the
last year had evaporated and the 'Old Katie' had come
back to life. Monkey couldn't stay mad at her for long
and eventually relaxed and laughed along with her.

'OK, let's try this again, shall we?' she said, once

she'd composed herself and refocused on the task ahead. She took her time this time and got used to the weight and balance of the oars and the feel of them as they cut through the water. She started rowing but you couldn't actually call it that at first. The boat slowly moved with a degree of clumsiness and she quickly learned how to dip and scoop the paddles through the surface, making a smoother flow. This was a lot more difficult than it looked. Every now and then the water would splash upwards if she didn't hit the surface quite right and the excess drops splashed them both. Monkey wasn't a fan and complained bitterly.

'What are you doing, you're soaking me?' he sulked.

'You try it, then – see if you can do any better,' she bit back with a snort. 'I'm trying my best.' She then dropped the oars back into the boat and folded her arms. 'I'm waiting.'

'All right, all right, I'm sorry Katie, I'm just nervous and scared for Shelley. I shouldn't be taking it out on you. You are doing your best, I can see that,' he apologised. As soon as Shelley's name was mentioned, it brought Katie back to her senses. This was a mission of life or death. There was no time for sulking.

'Ok then.' She tried again and the boat slowly started moving, gliding across the smooth surface of the water instead of jerking. She even began to enjoy it after a while. Monkey also began to relax and things fell into place. As she got closer to the area where she thought she'd originally entered the river, she eased off. She made sure she was a little further upstream so they could slowly drift over the landing area. She and Monkey looked over either side – starboard and port.

They gazed unconvincingly into the darkened mass of water with more hope than actual expectation. It was really too murky to see anything and they both knew it, but neither uttered a word for a while. They looked with great concentration at anything that resembled an unusual stone. The only thing they could really see for sure was the disc-like shape of the moon's reflection overhead. Every now and then, there would be a sharp intake of breath, followed by a sigh. Monkey turned to the starboard side and stared as hard as he could and Katie switched to port. Monkey's head and eyes hurt from constantly staring at a blank canvas, but he wouldn't relent.

'Katie,' he whispered at first; his echoed voice hissed across the vastness of the river. But she was too engrossed in finding the stone herself to hear him.

'Katie!' Monkey blurted a lot louder this time, disturbing the serenity of the moment.

'What!' she replied sharply and twisted herself round to where he was slumped. 'Look, I don't want to miss anything, so be quick,' she hissed.

'Look! I've found something,' he instructed and pointed his finger.

'What is it, where...?' she said and moved over to the same side, feeling a little unconvinced. The boat listed, but only to a certain point. Monkey nodded and dabbed his finger almost into the water, his eyes bright with excitement. Then she saw it! It was deep inside the gloomy and murky world of the river. It was dim and distant, but it was there . . . a small, glowing pebble. Could that be it, she pondered. She stared harder and the more she looked, the more convinced she became. Monkey forgot all about his fear for a moment and beamed a huge smile.

'That's it, Katie, that's it,' he chirped excitedly and, forgetting himself, almost jerked overboard. Katie grabbed him before he did. He sighed heavily and swallowed hard.

'It's the stone . . . it's the stone,' he repeated.

'But it could be anything, Monkey. We can't just assume it's our stone. We have to get hold of it first to make sure,' she said trying not to get both their hopes up for nothing.

'I'm going to have to climb in and swim to it,' she said reluctantly. Before she could disrobe, a strange thing happened – the stone dimmed and moved. Monkey stared in bewilderment.

'Did you see that, Katie? Look, it's moving.'

'Wha . . . How? It can't be.' She stopped what she was doing and stared at the light. It *was* moving. Not only that, but it was also darting here and there. There was a long pause of thought.

'What just happened? How could it move? It's a stone. It can't be *our* stone then, can it? Stones don't move on their own, Monkey, it must be a glowing fish of some kind.'

'Anything is possible in Reflections. *You* know that, Katie,' Monkey said. Katie couldn't figure it out, nor could Monkey, until things became a lot clearer. The dim light came closer to the surface.

'What the hell is this thing doing?' Katie cursed, to the utter amazement of Monkey. The closer it got to the surface, the more convinced they were it was their precious stone, but hope turned to tragedy. They could then see why it was moving. It was, indeed, *their* brooch and it wasn't being transported along by the current. It was inside the belly of a medium-sized fish!

'Good grief, that fish has eaten our stone,' Monkey announced with astonishment as it poked its head above the water.

'Dah, well, you think?' Katie responded sarcastically. Monkey gave her a steely look and even in the faded light of evening, Katie could see its meaning. The fish swam close to the boat and Katie lent out to try and catch it.

'This is a gift, Katie, grab it now,' he insisted. But this fish didn't want to be caught and duly avoided their attention. It began to swim away freely, as if mocking them.

'Damn and blast – it's getting away, Katie; smack it with the oar,' Monkey shouted, nodding to the one next to her right knee.

'I don't see *you* doing much, *you* smack it,' she shouted, but it was too heavy for him and she could see it was up to her. So she lifted it up and aimed it at the fish as it swam away. She thrashed it down with a huge SMACK! But it missed the fish completely. The fish continued, untroubled by its pursuers and zig-zagged its way ever onward. This left a disgruntled animal and human cursing in its wake. By the time Katie had grappled and re-slotted the oars back into position, the fish was almost out of sight.

'Come on Katie, come on, don't let it get away.' Calls of encouragement from her animal friend soon spurred her into pursuit and they were flowing along at a rate of knots. Katie dipped and thrust her way along the quietly-rolling, glassy, river. Heave, heave, heave. She could hear the words pummelling inside her head. They were almost within a boat and a half's length of the fish, which seemed to be playing with them. Only a few more strokes and Katie would be really close to its tail. It was the Oxford and Cambridge boat race all over again. As she approached, Monkey eased over the side and thrust his hand into the water. But the crafty fish dropped down deeper into the darkened depths and was swallowed up by an underground crevice.

'Blast that crafty little devil. He knows we're after him,' Monkey barked. The pair looked on in dismay as the glowing fish swam out of sight. The boat drifted on with momentum and eased past until it slowed to the pace of the river. Exhausted, Katie slumped back into the row boat and buried her face in her hands. She was devastated, but couldn't speak in between panting.

What were they going to do now? The fish had gone below ground with her only chance to help Shelley; could things get any worse? All the excitement of the chase subsided and the tranquil surroundings returned to normal.

'Oh, my god,' Katie uttered, her rather croaky voice shattering the silence. She sat upright. 'That's it. It's all over.' And she began to sob in a pool of self-pity.

'Katie.' Monkey's soft tone filtered through her thoughts. 'It'll be all right, we'll find it somehow,' he said, hoping to comfort her but knowing full well it was hopeless.

'Oh shut up, Monkey,' she cried rudely, erupting back at him through her tears. He was taken aback.

'It's gone and you know it.' Her tears were now replaced by anger.

'There's no need to take it out on me, young lady,' he uttered defensively, and turned away. 'I'd forgotten how childish you can be,' he retorted. Katie puffed a long uneasy stream of air from her half-open mouth and clenched her eyes shut. It wasn't his fault. It was hers. She shouldn't take it out on him, she thought.

'I'm sorry, Monkey, I didn't mean it, honestly! But how can we possibly get it back? I mean, I've lost everything and haven't got a clue where Shelley is either. It's hopeless.' Monkey glanced back at her and caught her eyes glistening from the moon's reflection.

'Don't cry, Katie, we'll figure it out. We'll have to do it without the stone. There *must* be a way somehow', he said, then smiled, which was difficult to see in the dim light.

'What do we do now then?' she questioned.

'Let's paddle back to shore and go back to my hut. We can get a nice hot drink and something to eat whilst we work on a plan. In the full light of day, things will seem easier. Who knows, we may even find Kevin.' He ended with a whiff of hope. She began laughing.

'Oh, this is hopeless,' she said, and Monkey looked at her in a state of befuddlement.

'Why are you laughing?' he asked. 'Are you mad?' Then he realised what he'd just said, considering she'd been under a psychiatrist for a year. 'Oops, sorry.'

'Well I'm supposed to be helping you, aren't I? That's why you sent for me, and here you are trying to make me feel better.' A smile curled her lip and even

Monkey could feel her happiness and friendship in the overwhelming darkness.

'Give me a hand, Monkey, let's get to shore,' she said with a renewed determination. 'That bloody fish was a tricky devil wasn't he?' Katie mused.

'Yeah, he was,' Monkey replied with a giggle. After a fair amount of paddling, they reached the bank, but it was densely black.

'Where are we, Monkey? I don't recognise anything. Do you?' Katie groped on the ground to find somewhere to tie the boat.

'I-I don't know Katie. Nothing feels familiar here.' He answered truthfully, trying to work out his whereabouts. 'It's way too dark even for *me* to get my bearings.'

'Give me a hand with this,' she urged, and the pair pulled the small craft to dry land.

'It'll be all right here,' Katie puffed and tied the rope to a heavy pebble. They moved off the pebbled banking and further on inland. The ground underfoot felt soft and dry but very uneven, which made moving around really difficult. They eventually clambered their way up to a different surface altogether – the loose, slippery shale of a quarry.

'Oh, great, this is going to be hard going! Two steps forward and three slips back. Let's turn back?' she groaned.

'We've come this far and it's pointless going back now. Let's plod on and find a cave or something,' he said in the darkness. Reluctantly she agreed and continued. It was again hard going in the dark, and unnerving because they had no idea which direction to head for. The two figures stumbled for quite a while uphill, until the slope levelled out.

'I don't recognise any of this, Katie; in fact, I don't think I've even been here before . . . we're lost!' he announced.

'Oh, good grief, could this get any worse? We're going to have to camp and sleep somewhere and find out where we are in the morning.' Katie moaned again, but a voice in the bleakness of night changed everything!

'Who is it dares to wake me?' The voice came thundering from below, and rippled the ground with a deadly force.

Chapter 5

Voice

Katie at first stood rigid like an exhibit in a museum, and then a ripple of fear racked her body. Monkey, on the other hand, was astonished and lost for words! They fumbled for each other's hand and clasped tightly.

'M-Monkey, what was that?' Katie whispered urgently through the dense blackness. Monkey was in stunned silence, which gave Katie even more goosebumps. She shook his hand vigorously.

'Monkey . . . Monkey, what are you sensing? Is there any . . .' Katie started to say, but was interrupted.

'WHO IS IT THAT WAKES ME?' The voice was more damning this time and impatient, its throaty wail vibrated the ground on which they stood. Katie screamed and her voice was swallowed up. She tightened her grip on Monkey and instinctively spread her other arm outwards in a bid to steady herself.

'Please don't hurt us. I'm K-Kati-tie...' she trembled, but couldn't get any more information out.

'I-I-I am M-M-Monk-k-key, your Highness,' Monkey cut in, stuttering uncontrollably as his nerves got the better of him. 'To whom do I speak?'

'You do not need to know that, you only speak when spoken to. I am in command here. This is my domain.' The controlling voice sliced through the night air like a sabre. It didn't have the deep, gritty feel of a man's voice – it was more of a female shriek. But a female that held absolute power. The more intense the timbre of the voice, the more the ground trembled as if the soil itself was as scared as they were.

'S-sorry, y-your Majesty.' Monkey apologised, tripping over his own tongue. Katie stood by silently, wondering what to do next. There was a small pause and then the voice boomed again.

'Girl, come closer,' the voice beckoned, but Katie didn't move. She physically shook and even took a step back. 'Come closer, I won't hurt you, I promise. Don't you think a being as powerful as I could have hurt you the instant you entered my domain? You're quite safe, now come forward.' The voice changed its pitch from abrasive to sombre. Katie did feel that the creature, if it wanted to, could have easily squashed her like a bug. Even though she didn't know what it looked like, or how big it could possibly be, surely something with a voice so powerful that it shook the very ground she stood on was capable of anything. So she relented and slowly moved a step closer. It was difficult. There was no reference point she could fix on, nothing that gave her a clue as to where she was stepping.

'B-but I c-can't see where I'm going a-and I might fall over,' she said honestly, still feeling the nerves.

'Ah, yes, it's dark up there, isn't it?' the voice echoed from below. 'I can soon sort that out.' There was a moment's silence and then a light appeared; a small, yellow glow at first that emitted from what looked like a fissure in the rock. The beam became stronger and changed into a shaft of amber that burst from the depths. The light had a warm feel that radiated towards Monkey and Katie. It illuminated the surrounding area, but not too much that it blinded; just enough so that Katie and Monkey could find their bearings. They were standing on the top of a slate mountain. The ground itself was fragmented like the pieces of a gigantic puzzle that spread in all directions and disappeared into the shadows. Monkey and Katie's bodies were outlined in yellow against the dense backdrop. The light spanned about ten metres or so, like a solid rainbow. In the background, there were piles of slated, obelisk towers that encircled the fissure like guards protecting their queen. Katie felt a little braver, now that she could actually see where she was going, and moved forward a few steps until she was parallel with Monkey. He was staring down into the depths of the rock scar.

'It's amazing, Katie,' he whispered as he looked hypnotically at the beautiful, luminous colour. She could see the reflection of the light painted on his glassy, marbled eyes. She, too, looked over the edge and tried to make out the source. There was little that either of them could see, especially as the light at the base was so strong. It wasn't just the light that drew them closer or the command of the enigma itself. It was also the warmth of it, and they bathed in its glow.

'That's quite far enough.' The great voice ripped through the earth. Katie was taken by surprise and the two of them stepped back. How could it know where she and Monkey were standing? There were no eyes to speak of. They hadn't even seen the body of the being, so how could it know? But it did!

'Move one step closer and no more, girl, and only you.' The voice was precise in its command. 'You will not be harmed.' It seemed to want not only to talk to her, but also keep her safe. Monkey smiled at her and gently patted her on the shoulder, and gave a gentle shove. He also gestured with a nod for her to do as she'd been asked.

'First you want me to come, then go back, now you want me to move forward again.' Katie complained in a mumbled whisper. She didn't understand what all this was about.

'Stop mumbling, girl, and do as I say,' the voice scolded. Katie did as she was told and took the one step that was asked. Some loose shale slipped forward and dropped over the edge.

'Tell me your name again, girl,' the faceless voice demanded.

'Katie, your Majesty, my name is Katie Hinge.' She was feeling braver and more relaxed. Monkey, in the quietest move he could muster, moved to Katie's side for moral support. He then slipped his trembling hand in hers.

'Welcome, Katie.' The voice lost its hard edge and was warming to its visitors. 'She said you would come and she was right.' Even though she couldn't see, Katie's eyes opened to their widest and she gripped Monkey's hand with new strength. He felt the pain, but knew he couldn't cry out, so he just gritted his teeth and winced.

'She, your Majesty?' It wasn't a direct question, but tastefully implied.

'Yes, she came and talked to me some nights ago,' the voice replied calmly.

'But who, your Highness, who is she? I don't understand.' Katie probed and waited as the voice pondered its answer, hoping beyond hope it was Shelley.

'I ask the questions here,' the voice reminded Katie.

'I understand and I apologise, your Majesty, but I have a friend in trouble and I need to know where she is.' Katie pushed with confidence.

'Shelley, she called herself, the same girl who came to me a year ago,' the voice continued. 'She didn't feel safe. She felt that something was watching her. She hoped you would come to find her.' Katie was bursting with questions.

'Who is watching her? Where can I find her now, your Majesty? She needs me. I need to help her.' Katie was almost ranting. In mid-flow, Monkey snatched his hand away from her grip and was blowing it tenderly.

'So many questions, little one. You have a vested interest in Shelley and you want to help her; I understand that.' The voice rebounded. 'Take your time and I'll answer what I can, but don't push me or I won't answer anything.' Katie felt a bond with the creature now.

'I'm so sorry, your Majesty, I'm just really worried about my friend and you're the last one to hear from her.' Katie took a pause and asked again. 'Please,' she said politely, 'can you tell me where I can find her? I would be most grateful.' The answer was short and ominous.

'You want to know one certain path that will lead to her?' she teased.

'Oh yes, your Majesty.'

'Below the mad witch's den is the only path you can take to find her.' The reply came almost as a riddle. Katie wrinkled her brow in thought.

'Wha . . .?' She was confused.

'The mad witch's den, the mad witch's den,' she repeated, 'there lays the only path.' Katie turned to Monkey and he shook his head and pursed his lips.

'I-I can't think, Katie.' He closed his eyes for a moment and she could see his eyes rolling underneath his lids. He was really trying to work this problem out, but to no avail.

'I don't know,' he answered honestly when he opened them again. Katie turned once more towards the hole in the rock.

'Where is that, your Majesty? Please tell me where it is?' Katie called, but there was no reply.

'Your Majesty? Hello? That isn't enough information. Please be more specific.' But Katie was only talking to herself and Monkey, and to add to this disappointment, the bright yellow light was dimming. The brilliance was ebbing back down the fissure from where it came.

'What's happening, Monkey? You can't leave it like this, your Majesty. We need to know where the mad witch's den is.' Katie was ranting and leaning further forward. 'Oh, don't go, I need to know. Please answer one more question,' she persisted, but everything was silent again and it didn't take long for the light to completely diminish . . . leaving them in darkness.

'Come back. Come back,' Katie shouted and stepped forward, but Monkey grabbed her arm. 'Please tell us,' she bellowed into the void; her voice echoed and evaporated.

'She's gone, Katie, and you'll be gone too if you go any further over. Come on, step back.' Monkey reasoned and he gently but firmly pulled her back to a safer distance from the edge. Katie knew it was useless to probe any more and she began to sob.

'Don't cry, Katie, I can't bear it when you cry. We must move on.' Monkey pleaded.

'Monkey, what do we do now? We still don't know where to go or how we're going to help her,' Katie asked in between sobbing and wiping the tears away with her sleeve. Monkey put his arm around her for comfort and warmth.

'Firstly, we have to go, Katie, and find shelter for the rest of the night. Then we have to work this problem out in the morning. We have been given a clue and you are good with clues, aren't you?' he insisted.

'I guess I am, but it seems like such a hopeless task,' Katie was babbling.

'I know, but rest and shelter first. Then we find the witch's den,' Monkey persisted. 'Come on Katie, gently now; let's get as far away from this place as possible.' So with arms linked, they helplessly scrambled across the loose slate of the quarry. The ground dipped into a slope and the pair steadily edged their way down to the bottom. It was hard going in the dark and very scary, too.

'I'm tired, Monkey,' Katie groaned, 'I need to sleep.' It was in the early hours that they left the rocky terrain and made their way along to the grassy lands of Reflections. By the light of the moon which poked its way from behind the clouds, they bore on. They walked almost in a trance-like state as fatigue and the mental stress took its toll. After an hour or so, they were both dead on their feet.

'Where are we, Monkey?' Katie asked sleepily.

'I don't know, but I think I've found somewhere to rest for the rest of the night.' He sounded excited. They found shelter eventually in a huge old tree with a hollowed trunk that was resting on its side, and had been for many years. The inner part had been ravaged by rot and time. The outer edge of bark was still intact and would keep out the wind and also keep them safe for now. Unbeknown to the two tired travellers, the ancient tree was set on a ridge overhanging the river. But they were too tired to even notice it. They scrambled over a large branch that partly obscured the entrance to the base of the tree and crawled inside.

'Here, Katie, we can rest here,' Monkey whispered, too exhausted to even talk loud. Katie didn't even argue. She positioned herself inside the hollow, wooded shelter and rolled up in a ball. Although it was summertime, it was still cold in the early hours. So it was warmer inside than out and the two of them slumped into a long, deep sleep. They would be hungry when they woke, but finding food and drink would be the least of their problems when dawn would finally break.

Far away, long into the distance, there were white flickers of sharp light, and behind them rumbles of thunder. A storm was coming, a storm that Reflections had never seen before, and Katie and Monkey were right in its path . . .

Chapter 6

Adrift

In the depths of slumber, Katie and Monkey were unaware of the sudden change in the weather outside. They were snuggled down inside the relative safety of their makeshift den, far away in dream. Being the middle of summer, the warmth absorbed from the day's rays were locked into the layers of bark. This made it warm and almost comfortable for the sleeping guests as the cold of early morning was banished.

It came, though, at first, fast and stealthy, like a silent assassin! The cold air mixed with the humid dry heat, tossed and swirled in the upper reaches of the atmosphere. The deadly combination of hot and cold whipped up into a violent force. Moisture formed into blackened rain clouds which emanated from the north, smothering an unsuspecting moon.

Heavily weighted with water, they finally released their payload. Rain lashed the ground in torrents, stabbing at the earth like a frenzied killer. Then, added to this, gusting winds that drove the rain earthwards with extra force. This explosive cocktail also brought with it thunder and lightning. The urgency of the deluge quickly saturated the dry, flaking soil that so needed to quench its thirst. The lightning itself clawed, gouged and tore at the land, setting fire to trees in the woodland. The sheer force of the wind followed and tore up the forests and countryside. The sheer power of the gale force winds soon unearthed the base of the hollowed log.

The fast-rising water seeped underneath the roots of the ancient tree and dislodged it from its moorings. The log slid smoothly through the muddied banking and onwards. The creaks and groans from the stretching skin of the moving timber woke the two travellers. But it was too late to escape by then.

'Monkey, Monkey, what's happening?' Katie repeated, as she screamed amidst the chaos. Their whole world seemed to revolve, literally, over and over like a tombola. They were each thrown tumbling with no time to recover. Katie slammed her head into the log wall, thus making her really dizzy, whilst Monkey tried with all his might to stay upright.

'Katie, hold on.' Monkey screeched as he tried to reach for her in the darkness, but it was impossible.

'Monkey, help. I feel sick,' she cried, but he could do nothing to help her. The trunk gathered momentum and, like a pair of trainers in a tumble dryer, the occupants were thrown from side to side. Katie was screaming uncontrollably as she thrashed around, trying to hold on. Monkey, though agile, was no match for the pounding log either.

The tree smashed into a rounded boulder on the river's edge and duly snapped in half with a giant crack. The force of the impact threw Katie and Monkey in different directions. They once again slammed into the smooth inners of the log. Katie threw up and consequently fell into her own vomit. She was crying and her body felt bruised. The log duly separated into two shorter lengths, both going in different directions. Luckily for them, they were in the same half. The two pieces impacted the water with an almighty splash and landed on their sides. Water immediately rose up inside the cylinder and the occupants were floating freely. Katie was left in a semi-conscious stupor, while Monkey was out cold. Still intact, it began to drift downstream, pulled along by the fast currents, like an oblong torpedo. The river water dispersed and the level inside dropped and its occupants were lucky not to drown. Most of the weight of the log, with its crippled limbs and thickened outer skin, was underneath and submerged. This kept it more balanced as it drifted along.

The raging storm finally began to weaken and the monster weather front began melting away into the background. Dawn was breaking, bringing the first light of morning and easing away the remains of the erratic summer squall. Thunder became less audible and the lightning became a pale glow in the distant hills. The rain also eased and subsided, paving the way for blue skies once more. The log floated helplessly down the open river, perfectly balanced but letting in water from both sides. Katie came round as the icy cold liquid seeped around her body. She was sat upright and her mouth was centimetres from above the surface. The cold temperature made her body tense. Where were they? She found it difficult to focus and her mouth was frozen shut. She coughed and spluttered through gritted teeth, unable to move them. She almost retched at the foul taste in her mouth. Luckily the water was receding, making it easier to move instead of fighting the current. She felt the underside of her jaw – it was numb.

I must have banged it, she said inside her head. Monkey, where was he? Outside was getting lighter and so she quickly searched for her friend, fearing the worst. She dog-paddled along the inside, desperately looking for her friend.

'Mmmmmookkky.' In her weakened and cold state, Katie couldn't move her jaw to call out. Her breathing became laboured and she took sharp breaths in and out like a machine gun. Where are you? Where are you? She screamed the words inside her mind. She knew in these temperatures that neither could last for much longer, even though it was the middle of summer. Hypothermia was already setting in; she knew because she remembered her swimming instructor lecturing her once about cold temperatures in rivers and seas. She needed to find Monkey and they desperately needed to get warm.

A little further over from her was what looked like a sodden ball of fluff, but it wasn't moving, which frightened her beyond words. She scrambled forward, half crawling and half doggy-paddling. Katie reached out and gripped what she hoped would be her best friend and hopefully alive. It was him! She grabbed his body as best she could and lifted his head above water. Her hands were getting numb and her legs felt as though they weren't even hers. Was he alive or dead? She didn't know. The water had fallen to just below her and Monkey's waists and she realised that she had to give him mouth-to-mouth. Number one she remembered from her coach was that she had to blow hard into his lungs – all this whilst pinching his nose – and then massage his heart. B-u-t she'd only done it to 'Sally', the plastic doll she'd practised with. This was different; this wasn't a plastic doll or a human for that matter. It was her best friend in this world, but also it was a monkey. Could she...k-i-s-s a monkey? Come on Katie, she told herself, you have to do this. But even as she plucked the courage to start the procedure, she remembered – her mouth was frozen shut! Suddenly the log jolted and a wave of river pushed its way through, lifting the water level. It was harder now trying to keep herself and Monkey afloat. On her own, she would have treaded water easily, but holding on to someone else was a lot more difficult. It was very strange the two of them bobbing in the water, but Mr Jones, her swimming instructor, had taught her well. But even so, holding someone's head above water was one thing in a swimming pool; but doing so in a slowly-rotating log, drifting down a river, was completely different. This was an experience they hadn't taught her in swimming class. She tried shaking him, hoping he would come round and hoping that he wasn't already dead! His body was holding heat even in the cold of the river water, so there was hope he could be still alive. And she thought she could feel a weak pulse, but that was difficult to read especially in these conditions. The only real thing she could do was to keep his head above water and hope that he hadn't swallowed much. The rotation kept knocking her off balance and therefore Monkey dipped regularly under the surface. As if that wasn't enough, every now and then the whole log slowly rotated clockwise, like the hour hand on a clock face. With the hollowed log facing downstream, she could see ahead and it scared her to death! The other half of the tree was further along, and to Katie's utter disbelief she saw it stop! It then jolted for a moment and fliped completely out of sight!

'Oh-my-god; Waterfall!' she said through clenched teeth. This day wasn't going to end with a happy outcome. The log twisted once again and rolled slowly, moving anti-clockwise this time, across the river, giving Katie a view of the banking each side.

There can only be seconds left, she thought. There's nothing I can do about this. She waited and closed her eyes. She waited – waited and waited! Then, strangely, calmness took hold; the quiet and serene calm of the seconds before a battle, or watching someone on a movie falling off a high building before impacting the bottom. 'You will always be my best fr . . .' There was a gigantic thud and the log stopped! Monkey and Katie were thrown against the log wall. The water level inside instantly and strangely began dropping, until it was only knee-deep. Katie was by now battered, bruised, cold and scared. Monkey still wasn't moving, but she propped him up in a sitting position. Where were they? They couldn't have gone over the edge. She and Monkey were still alive and not thrashing around in deep water, or smashed to smithereens on the rocks. There was a knot-hole in the bark, about the size of an apple, beside her head. She clenched her eyes tight shut at first and then reluctantly looked through and reeled back in disbelief.

'Mookey, Mookey, wwwake ubbb!' she pleaded as she tried to wake him, but he was still out cold. She felt for his pulse again and was relieved when it throbbed away stronger than before. For the first time, though, she felt totally alone. Her stomach felt as though it was made of rubber and was being slowly twisted. The cold water, mixed with her nerves, made her shake in spasms. Feeling was coming back to her jaw, ironically, and so began to chatter. Peering through the hole once more brought on the reality of her predicament. Besides the sheer white curtain of water being violently sucked downwards, there was also the thirty or so metre drop to the basin below. From side to side, the relentless flow of the river pushed onwards, slowly chipping away at the fragile log's exterior. This place of safety was disintegrating before her eyes and there was no way out. The log must be wedged she thought, and she shakily stood up and walked to one end. Through various gaps in the bark she could see that the log was precariously jammed against some boulders. At random intervals, there were jolts impacting the side of the log like missiles. The storm had loosened debris in the shape of tree limbs which were being washed down river. There was nowhere else for it all to go so it was heading for the log jam. It was only going to be a matter of time before the log would smash completely into pieces or topple over into the abyss below! She stood as close to the edge as possible.

'Help. Someone please help us.' Her jaw relaxed, she shouted in the remote hope of someone being close by. But even if they were, how were they going to get them out? It was a deadly situation. She turned and looked at her friend who was hopelessly oblivious to their plight.

'Oh, Monkey, we can't help Shelley now. There is no way out of this. Shelley, please forgive me, I did try, honestly.' She walked back to where Monkey was slumped and put her arm around him and started sobbing. Huge tears rolled down her muddied face as she hugged him for all she was worth.

'I'm so sorry, Shelley,' she repeated.

Chapter 7

Certain Death

The log was perched precariously on the edge of the waterfall and ready to tip over at any given moment. Monkey was still unconscious, slumped against the side like a discarded rag. Katie couldn't think straight. How on earth am I going to get out of this; the words tumbled in her mind. The only thing that was helping was the fact that the water level had dropped to below waistline. So, whilst sitting, she lifted her friend into her arms and snuggled him close. She eased forward to get a better look outside, to get another look at the trouble they were in. She cradled Monkey like a baby, trying to get him to come around, and also to keep them both warm for survival. She was still shaking with cold, but the sheer drop and the white vapour haze that rose up to halfway made her shake even more! Her eyes glazed over and she began gently sobbing at first and then a full-blown barrage of tears. Her sobbing and trembling brought Monkey out of his dreamlike state. He lifted his eyes towards Katie's and squinted into focus. She was so engrossed in self-pity that she didn't even see him looking at her. His head throbbed and his throat burned and he didn't even know if he could say anything, but he tried.

'Ka-tie . . .' he squeaked, but it brought on a fit of coughing and he spat up a mouthful of river water. Katie realised that he was conscious and burst back into life.

'Monkey! Monkey! You're all right. You're all right,'

she repeated, in between wiping the tears away with her sodden sleeve.

'Yes . . . yes, I appear . . . to . . . uh, to be,' he finally managed to gasp. 'Where are we?' he asked, trying to make sense of his surroundings. As soon as he blurted the words, Katie recalled the situation they were now presented with.

'Oh, Monkey, you don't want to know. It's hopeless. You really don't want to know where we are,' she said with trepidation, 'There's no way out.' Then there was a thud and an almighty jerk and the log shifted forward. Katie screamed and Monkey's black eyes widened and it brought on more coughing.

'We're going to die, Monkey.' Katie screeched as she stared into his eyes.

'Oh, shut up Katie and help me up!' He was angry. 'Come on, help me up and stop messing about.' He commanded, 'We're not going to die. Get that thought out of your head and stop crying. Everything seems hopeless until you've figured a way out. You know that, there's always a way out.' There was a determination to his voice and this made her stop moping instantly!

'I know it looks a grave situation, but we've gone through tougher scrapes than this before, girl.' He looked at her. 'Haven't we?' Katie took a moment to think, rolled her eyes and nodded her head gently.

'Yes, I suppose we have,' she said softly and calmly.

'Which bank are we closest to?' Monkey asked, peering from end to end. Katie seemed to be rejuvenated and sprang into action.

'This side, I think,' she said, pointing to one end of

the log. They made their way to one open end and as they got to the edge, everything was put into perspective. The bank was approximately eight metres away. They were on the cusp of the waterfall and the distance between them and safety wasn't that bad. But the water between the log and the banking was still heavy and pushing hard downstream. They looked on in despair; it was way too strong a current to try and wade across. Monkey looked around for something to help, but he was honest with himself when he realised there was nothing.

'We'll never make it.' Katie responded woefully. 'It's too far and the water is moving way too fast. We'll be washed straight over the edge and end up smashed down there.' She looked into the haze of frothing white water. Monkey looked over again and gulped in the back of his throat. Really speaking, he did agree with her, but he couldn't let her know that. Katie grasped hold of him and lifted him up in a sort of hug.

'Katie, is this the right time to be thinking of a farewell hug?' he asked.

'Shut up,' she ordered while she was holding him. He could see she was thinking of something. In her mind it was like holding a baby, maybe a little heavier, but not too heavy. She knew this because she'd babysat a couple of times for her next-door neighbour and he was roughly about the same weight.

'Monkey, I know a way out of this.' She was certain and determined.

'I know, Katie, we can do it. What's your plan?' He was excited.

'No, I'm serious, Monkey. This is not a heroic

speech – I actually think I know a way of getting us out of this mess.' Monkey realised that she'd worked something out.

'Go on then, tell me!' he said. 'Don't keep me in suspense.' She paused.

'I'm going to throw you.' She made the statement and waited for a reply, but one wasn't forthcoming. Monkey looked at her in a weird way.

'What! You're going to throw me, where – over there?' He pointed the distance from the log to the nearest point of the land.

'Yes.' Katie's answer was short.

'You're not, you know,' he answered sharply.

'It's the only way. Can't you see? I throw you, and you go and get some rope or vine to rescue me. Then you come back and pull me to safety.' He stopped and thought for a moment. It *did* make sense, but then he realised that the log wouldn't last that long. He tried to deter her.

'But what if you don't throw me far enough?' He waited for her answer.

'Then I'll have to get another Monkey.' She looked at him with a menacing grin. He could do nothing but giggle. She stopped abruptly and her attention was caught by something else.

Something caught her eye and she squinted into the tree-line.

'Katie, Katie, what are you thinking of now – a big slingshot and me as the ammunition?' he said comically.

'Can you see that, oh, good grief, it-it can't be.

Please let it be!' she uttered in total disbelief.

'What is it, Katie?'

'It's Kevin. Kevin, is that really you?' She called out with tingling excitement, even hope in her voice and she waved frantically at the person on the river bank.

'Kevin, Kevin, Kevin...Yahoo.' Monkey bellowed.

'Are you two all right?' he shouted back, his voice echoing across the hiss of the river.

'Yes, but as you can see, we're stuck here. I don't know how long this log will hold out,' she cried. There was a pause and no answer came while they waited. To Katie's dismay, he disappeared.

'Kevin, no, don't go! Where are you going? Kevin, come back,' she shrieked.

'Katie, he's probably gone for help or something,' Monkey said in support. Katie, though, didn't take her eyes from the banking. There was another humongous crunch and some more bits of the log fell over the edge. Both Katie and Monkey tried to steady themselves.

'Come on, Kevin, we haven't much time,' she ranted.

Soon, Kevin returned and he was carrying something that they, from a distance, couldn't make out straight away. Then it dawned on them that it was a bow.

'What's he going to do, kill us before we go over the edge?' she joked bitterly.

'Move back inside the log as far as you can,' Kevin instructed, as loud as he could, and the stranded pair did as they were asked. It felt even more obscure looking at this small figure through the circle of the log. Kevin attached a length of rope to an arrow by a thick piece of string. He'd already cut a small groove in the arrow's shaft so that the string wouldn't slide whilst in flight. He was ready! He raised the bow above his head and pulled back on the gut. The small rope pulled at the arrow as the rest of it lay coiled on the ground beside him. Trying to gauge its distance he finally let go and the arrow shot toward the roof of the log, but plonked into the water, way off its target.

'Damn it,' he cursed. The rope, he realised, was so heavy it pulled at the arrow and tugged it away from the desired area. He quickly reeled it back in and shook off the excess water. He carefully placed it back into position and raised it once more. Taking the strain he pulled back and realigned his target allowing for the calculation of the weight and drag. Once again he let go and watched as it veered to the right, not so far this time, but still missed the log.

'Bloody arrow,' he cursed again. He had considered himself a fine shot with a bow, but this was proving to be a hard test of his skill. He also realised that the log wasn't going to stay lodged there much longer either.

'What's happening, Kev?' Katie called from inside the wooden cylinder. Kevin bit his lip in annoyance.

'Katie, let him concentrate,' Monkey told her. This time, Kevin reeled the arrow back out of the water and jerked it back into the bow. He raised it for a third time and then thought for a moment and told himself to relax. He took a deep breath, took the strain and let go . . . swoosh. It shot through the air and landed smack on target, burying itself in the meaty skin of the log.

'Yes!' he said, congratulating himself. 'OK, tie the rope to the log somehow and I can get you over to me,' he said excitedly. The water hadn't risen any higher inside the log and so Monkey and Katie waded over to the end. The point of the arrow had gone almost all the way through the wood. The trouble was the wood was so rotten that tying it was going to be a problem.

'Send Monkey across first,' Kevin called. Yeah that would make sense, Katie thought because of his weight. He was obviously a lot lighter than her as she remembered her first plan. She pulled at the arrow and, worryingly, it came through easily, with the rope still hitched to it.

'If I hold the rope as tight as I can this end, Monkey should easily climb across.' Katie shouted over the river.

'No, Katie, you go first,' Monkey insisted. 'I'm not leaving you behind.'

'Monkey, listen! With you and Kevin holding the rope for me, I have more chance of getting across,' she said, actually making a lot of sense. Monkey was impressed.

'When did you get all intelligent on me?' he asked sarcastically. She smiled back and said nothing.

'Go on, up you go,' she said, pushing him towards the rope. He climbed up and hung upside down. He did shimmy along quite easily to the end. Climbing was second nature to him, being a monkey. Now it was Katie's turn!

'I have nothing to tie it to. You'll just have to pull me, Kev,' she called tentatively.

'All right then, tie it around your waist and make sure it's secure,' he instructed. Katie did as she was asked and gingerly stepped off the log and on to a stone. But she slipped and instantly fell straight into the water and was immediately pushed against the rocks with the force. She was slightly winded, but felt a lot better when she could feel the bottom. The pair on shore pulled on the rope with all their might. Katie scrambled against the flow of water and was, bit by bit, pulled along the rocks. All was going well until she came to the end of the rocky perimeter. There was a gap of about three metres between the end of the rocks and the banking.

'I-I can't make it. I-I'll get washed over,' she cried, still trying to hold on.

'We won't let you go, honestly; now come on,' Kevin shouted. Both Monkey and Kevin pulled hard on the rope. Katie waded forward, but immediately with the force of the water again was washed straight over the edge and out of sight. They couldn't see or hear her, but the tension on the rope was strong.

'Pull, Monkey, pull.' Kevin screeched frantically, but nothing. They heaved again, their grip slipping. This time, Katie's head appeared through the sheen of the water's glassy surface. She wasn't moving and this spurred them to pull frantically with all their might. There was a huge CRACK! The log had dislodged, as another heavy lump of debris had washed downstream and impacted its flank. The two huge tree trunks tumbled over the water's edge as Kevin and Monkey looked on in horror! Did they hit her or not? They couldn't tell.

'Pull, pull, Monkey,' Kevin screamed, as they realised they had, in fact, missed Katie by a matter of metres. She was dangling like a clock pendulum; the rope was snagged on a rock.

'Monkey, pull harder or we'll lose her,' Kevin shouted frantically. With a sudden burst of energy, they tugged it once again and released it. They soon had her on the banking and pulled her to safety. She was shaking with cold, but she was breathing. All three of them fell back and rested in the warmth of the morning sun.

Chapter 8

A Band of Three

The hiss of the waterfall was still buzzing in her ears, but Katie was too exhausted to open her eyes. She'd been lying on her left side and eventually flipped over on to her back and gasped a long, concentrated sigh. Every sinew of her body was crying out in pain. Everything ached, even her teeth for some reason. She cracked open her tired eyes and moved her mouth to speak. She saw Kevin first, who stood over her with his finger to his lips. She could just make out his facial features against the sun, almost silhouetting his outline.

'Don't speak – get your breath back first, Katie,' he uttered in a slow, soft whisper. The sun was high and the warmth of it flowed through her like an anaesthetic, healing as it warmed. It was lovely, tranquil, like heaven, she supposed. She didn't have the strength to move for a while and just lay there.

The urgent rush of water still raced below, but she wasn't in any immediate danger now and it lulled her back into a dreamy sleep.

'Katie, Katie. Wake up. Come on, girl.' The melodic tone of Monkey seeped into her watery dream. She wasn't drowning; she was floating alone on an air bed, slowly slurping on an ice lolly. 'You were whimpering in your sleep.' She opened her eyes and saw the small, round, leathered face and beady eyes of Monkey, peering back. A huge smile filled both their faces and he knelt down by her side and hugged her.

'Monkey, we're OK, thank goodness.' He nodded gleefully in agreement.

'It was touch and go there for a moment though, Katie,' he said. She smiled and sniffed the air with gusto. There was a fantastic aroma of fish cooking somewhere and her stomach rumbled. She grasped her belly and groaned.

'Ah, that smells lovely,' she gushed, closing her eyes and conjuring up the picture of newspaper-wrapped fish and chips.

Her stomach gurgled again and she yawned in a bid to disguise it. Monkey grinned.

'Hungry?' he said simply and she nodded vigorously. 'Kevin's here and he's been cooking something special.'

Behind Monkey loomed the bigger, masculine frame of her old friend Kevin. It had been a year since she'd seen him and in all that time he'd certainly changed. He was taller and much more a man than a boy, with the same strikingly handsome face. But his jawline was narrower and more pronounced, defining his cheekbones. Johnny Depp, she first thought. He still kept his stubby nose, but his eyes were brown, the colour of chocolate.

Katie paused for a moment and then came back to reality. She checked herself from staring at him, because in her mind the word 'Lush' came bursting through. As far as she knew, Kevin was Shelley's and she didn't want to get involved. But he *is* hot, she thought. He turned to face her and beamed a smile.

'Sleep well?' he said, also with a grin that nearly made her melt.

'Yeah-yeah, yes, thanks. You look good, oh, uh, sorry, I mean it's good to see you, Kevin.' The words just slipped out and her face began reddening. 'Thank you so much for rescuing us, Kevin. It was really frightening. I thought that was it,' she said solemnly.

'It'll happen one day I suppose, but not today,' he said sounding like a philosopher.

'Come on then, Katie, let's eat, but take it easy.' He moved towards her and reached out, gently lifting her arm. 'Do you think you're strong enough to try and eat something?' he asked.

'Most definitely, I'm starving. Uh, I mean I could eat something, I suppose.' She was a little too excited and tried to calm herself.

'Monkey, you hungry?' he asked. Monkey was sitting in the background while these two were catching up with each other.

'Yes, thank you, Kevin. I'll have a bite,' he said coolly.

She eventually got to her feet, but with a bit of a wobble at first. The river had sapped her strength. It felt like a scene from Bambi. She closed her eyes for a moment, righted herself and breathed in, and was ready.

'Wow, take your time,' Kevin urged.

'Give me a sec,' she said and breathed deeply again. It seemed to steady her. Another big sigh and it made her stronger somehow. 'OK, I'm ready.' She let Kevin guide her to his camp, which was only a matter of twenty or so metres.

'Oh, that wonderful smell; mmmmmmm,' she exclaimed. Good-looking and he can cook: she tried to keep her thoughts to herself.

'Not hungry, then?' Kevin joked as he sat her down by the side of the glowing fire. There, nestled on the flames, was a large frying pan and inside, sizzling away, was a crispy, golden fish. To Katie's right, Monkey sat down and on his lap was a metal plate, ready to be filled.

'You don't waste any time, do you?' Katie teased, with mouth wide open. Monkey shrugged his shoulders awkwardly and grimaced, which made Katie chuckle. Soon, Kevin was serving up the best fish steaks that Katie and Monkey had ever eaten. They all tucked in without saying a word until all that was left were the bones. Katie put her plate to one side and slumped back against a tree stump.

'Oh, I'm stuffed,' she announced, patting her stomach. 'Thank you so much, Kev.'

'That's OK. Now that lunch is over, I would like to ask a few questions. Is that all right?' he probed.

'Yeah, carry on,' Katie said, with a wave of her hand.

'Right, first things first then,' he said, as if ready for a speech. 'When and how did you get here, Katie?' Kevin questioned. He was sitting opposite the both of them and eased back on to his elbows.

'That would be me, Kevin, I called her,' Monkey cut in sharply. 'We needed help and I knew she would come right away, knowing Shelley was in trouble.'

'Why? We could have handled this on our own,' Kevin probed again sharply. Katie was stunned for a second and then retaliated.

'Because,' Katie said sternly. 'You seem to forget, Kevin, that Shelley was my friend long before she was yours or anybody else's in Reflections.' Her face wrinkled in annoyance and her lids closed around her now narrowed eyes. 'Why shouldn't I come here? I'm annoyed that you never considered asking me before, Kevin. I can help. A problem shared is a problem halved,' she said, remembering her mother's old saying.

'She's right you know, Kev.' Monkey looked at Kevin and smiled.

'All right then, you *do* know that Lord Fairbourne and Shadrack are both dead,' he said firmly. 'It's a dangerous place here in Reflections.' He peered at Katie as if to say you'd be safer back where you belong.

'What's your problem, Kevin? Have I done something to upset you?' Katie said, and added, 'Why *shouldn't* I be here?'

'I don't want you to get hurt,' he said honestly, and looked more relaxed.

'I can look after myself,' she snapped back. 'Me and Monkey can go on alone if you don't want us involved with you. We'll find Shelley eventually and sort things out.'

'No, that's not it, Katie. Look, I *do* want you here, honest. Sorry, I'm just worried, worried about Shelley,' he said with a frown.

'We all are, Kev. That's why I'm here. That's why Monkey called me in the first place. We can all help each other.'

'Anyway, besides that, how did you know we were

in the river?' Monkey cut in, trying to change the way the conversation was going. Kevin paused.

'I didn't really know you were in the river, that was just luck. I've been trying to find some clue as to where Shelley has gone. I was hungry and decided to get some food and rest before I looked further. I was fishing before the storm took hold and I just about caught the fish we just ate before the river swelled,' he said.

'That was one tasty fish, Kevin.' Monkey exclaimed. Kevin smiled and looked at the two of them.

'What . . .' they announced in harmony. They looked at each other and back at Kevin.

'Are you missing something, something really important?' he asked, with eyes that were clearly hiding a secret.

'This was inside it. This was inside the fish.' He held it out in his upturned palm and produced the jewel.

'Oh my . . . oh my god.' Katie was lost for words, the relief on her face was monumental. 'I don't believe it. That is nuts.' She was gobsmacked.

'That was the fish we were trying to catch yesterday,' Monkey said disbelievingly. 'That's got to be a billion-to-one chance,' he said in wonder. 'It swallowed the stone and you caught it.'

'Could I have it back, please, Kevin?' There was a real desire there and she picked it out of his hand and took a long look at its sparkly exterior. 'I never thought that I would see you again,' she whispered to it.

'Where were you two going, anyway? Especially trying to travel in that rotten log,' he asked.

'We didn't intend to travel in the log, Kev.' She shook her head. 'First of all, we tried to find the fish and get the stone back, after I'd dropped the stone in the river. The fish must have found it and swallowed it,' Katie began, still smiling, but her eyes glazed in remembrance. 'We went back to shore empty handed and got lost in the dark. We stumbled across a Voice in the darkness.' Kevin soon sat up to take note.

'You talked to the Voice in the Void?' he said, shaking his head, his eyes wide with wonder.

'Yes, why? Have you been there, too?' Katie was astonished.

'Yeah, me and Shelley back last time,' he remembered. 'What did she say this time?'

'She told us that the answer to our search was to be found under the mad witch's den. She said that Shelley had visited her days before, too.' Katie still looked baffled at the statement she'd just made.

'Wow, she never said. Which mad witch would that be?' Kevin said in confusion.

'How many mad witches are there in Reflections?' Katie said mockingly.

'We don't know who the voice meant,' Monkey added.

'Hold on,' Kevin said, scratching his head. 'Not Mad Maisey? But she's not a witch, she's just a mad old woman. And, anyway, I think she's dead now.'

'Oh no,' Monkey gasped in sheer terror and looked directly at Katie. Katie stared back in sympathy.

(In the previous year, when Katie and Monkey were trying to escape Shadrack Scarrat, they were

separated and Monkey was kidnapped by an odd old woman everyone in Reflections called Mad Maisey. She imprisoned Monkey in a cage and was going to boil him alive and eat him, before Katie burst in and rescued him).

'Don't worry, Monkey, you're safe this time, especially if she really is dead.' Katie gave an uncertain smile, which didn't give him much confidence.

'But if the voice told you this, then it must be true and that's where we have to go,' Kevin said. 'Everything she told me and Shelley was true, so we should go to Mad Maisey's house. But I don't know where it is.'

'Look, are we sure this Mad Maisey is the mad witch?' Kevin nodded quickly.

'Then if we all agree that Maisey is a witch, Monkey and I know where her house is.' Katie looked at her friend and then at Kevin. Monkey began to tremble.

'I-I can't go back there, Katie.' He began shaking violently. Katie put her arm around his shoulder and snuggled him. Kevin looked on in curiosity.

'I know you're scared,' she whispered so that only he could hear. 'I am, too. But this is for Shelley.' She nodded and he gazed back into her eyes. He dropped his head and thought.

'OK, for Shelley,' he relented and lifted his head again. She squeezed his shoulder gently.

'We should leave while it's still light.' Kevin broke the moment. 'How far is it from here?' he said, and looked at the both of them.

'I don't know. Where are we?' Monkey asked, trying to get his bearings. Katie got up and squinted through the trees.

'Is that the old railway line over there?' She partially cupped her hand over her brow to shade her eyes.

'I think so, why?' Kevin asked.

'Then if we follow the line so far, I think I can find Maisey's cottage.' She looked very pleased with herself. 'Remember the crash we had with the carriage, Monkey?'

'How could I forget, you nearly killed me!' he said, remembering as if it were yesterday.

'I think if we find the crash site, I can work it out from there.'

'OK then, are we all ready?' Kevin was impatient to leave.

'I don't know if I'll ever be ready to go back there,' Monkey said honestly.

'Me neither,' Katie added.

'What's with you two? She's just an old woman,' Kevin said.

'Not *any* old woman, Kevin. She tried to kill me last time,' Monkey remembered, but Kevin laughed.

'What, *that* old bat?' he said, still chuckling. 'She was as harmless then as she is now.'

'I hope she is dead, Kev, because if she's not, I'm telling you she's not a defenceless old woman, believe me,' Katie said, nodding.

'Look, let's find her house and see if we can find some clue to where Shelley is being kept.'

'I'll leave all my stuff here; nobody comes here so

it's safe enough,' Kevin said, packing some things away in a tent hidden inside some bushes. Then all three headed towards the railway line.

Chapter 9

Below the witch's den

Katie, Monkey and Kevin arrived at the farmhouse by early evening. The warmth of summer smiled upon the lonely cottage. It looked a little downtrodden on the outside with its dusty windows masking the interior. The thatched roof looked as threadbare as an old carpet. The garden was overgrown and matched the scruffiness of the building itself.

'This place hasn't seen much action in a while, by the look of things.' Kevin said, as he continued walking towards the door and then stopped suddenly, realising he was on his own. He spun round to find Katie and Monkey glued to the spot beyond the boundary line of the wall. They were mesmerised at the sight of the old building again. Kevin stood confused for a moment or two, and wrinkled his brow in annoyance. Then he glared at them with both barrels of his steely eyes.

'Come on, you two, we'll never find Shelley at this rate,' he grunted impatiently. Katie looked at Monkey with frightened eyes, but he was too transfixed to notice her gaze. She peered at Kevin as he was preparing to utter another word of protest. She shook her head in warning, in a bid to stop him. He looked awkward at first and then begrudgingly understood her insistence and held back.

'Monkey,' she gently whispered in his right ear, 'Monkey, it'll be all right this time. She isn't there. She's dead. I'm sure of it. I don't know why I know, it's just a feeling. You can see for yourself that the

85

house has been untouched.' She smiled at him and her eyes were beaming with warmth. Monkey craned his neck and gave her a solemn look, a troubled look, a look of fear and anxiety of the memories that the house brought back.

'I know she's dead, Katie. I can't feel her here, but I still find it hard to even think about going in. That day . . .' he responded.

'Shh. I totally understand, I was there too, remember.'

'Oh Katie, if you hadn't been there that day, who knows what would have happened.' He recoiled.

'Don't think like that, Monkey. I *was* there, wasn't I?' she continued with sympathy, 'Maybe, if only Kevin and I went in, perhaps that would be a better idea. Don't you think? Why go through it all again?' Kevin was looking hard at Katie and bursting to get on. She squinted at him in his impatience and scolded him with a harsh look. 'I honestly don't mind, Monkey,' she insisted.

'No Katie, we started this together and we'll finish it together. I called you, remember? I've *got* to do this.' He stood firm and nodded as if he'd wrestled with it and agreed in his own mind.

'Are we ready now?' Kevin persisted, this time with venom.

'Yes, Kevin, we are.' Katie gave him another scowl. 'He just needed a moment,' she said, shrugging her shoulders. 'You've absolutely no sympathy in that head of yours for anyone, have you?' She felt anger building up inside.

'That's not true and you know it. I feel very deeply that Shelley is safe,' he snarled, puffing out his chest.

Men, she said, in the recess of her mind. He turned away and made a move towards the heavy wooden door and pushed at it. It didn't budge, which made him even more annoyed! He leant against it with his shoulder and heaved; it began to give way.

'It hasn't been opened for quite some time; it's almost sealed itself. That should be a good sign, Monkey. If it hasn't been used, then she *must* be dead,' Katie assumed. There was a sharp CRACK, like the sound of a stick being snapped! And a long, piercing yawn as the door opened to its widest. Initially, it was darkest just inside the doorway and long, wispy, grey cobwebs loosely floated down from the ceiling. There was an uninviting screen of freshly disturbed dust particles that caught the light from the dirty windows. This made Katie cough and choke at first.

'I don't like this,' she whispered. The dirty windows didn't allow the full light of day inside. The gloom made for a very eerie setting, and what made things worse was distant scratching in the walls. They all nervously walked in and Monkey stopped with a shudder. He gulped down a huge swallow of saliva. His face creased in fear and he put his hand to his mouth. There, still hanging from the ceiling, was the cage that had imprisoned him a year ago; but it seemed a lot more recent in his mind. Katie gave his shoulder a squeeze of support. He turned towards her and gave a weak smile, his black eyes troubled.

'Come on,' she whispered, 'it'll be all right,' and as she said it, he felt her warmth.

'Where is it? It's got to be here somewhere.' Kevin burst into a fit of anger and tore around the room searching frantically for the entrance to the chamber below. 'This is ridiculous, it's not here,' he barked angrily. He turned to Katie. 'You've been misinformed. It's not here and she's not here.' He shot her a glare as if it were her fault.

'Kevin, calm down,' she snapped. 'You're just like a spoilt child. Good grief; we all miss Shelley and we all want to find her. Give it a chance – we've only just got here. Have some patience, will you, you madhead?' she said abruptly as if she were his mother. Monkey gave a hidden smirk, which took his mind off the house for a moment.

'Look, the Voice said it's here, so it must be here. Why would it need to lie? It was trying to give us a clue, you know, so we can find her, maybe?' she explained sarcastically. He looked at her whilst wiping a cobweb from his hair. He was hot, and sweat seeped from his scalp, down his neck, which made him itch.

'Well, if you can find it, show it to me then?' He folded his arms and stepped back, his face a picture of self-importance. He was really beginning to get on both Katie and Monkey's nerves. His handsome features were really forgotten and the admiration she held dissolved.

'You can be such a tool sometimes, Kev,' she said bluntly. 'OK, right, where would it be,' she mumbled to herself. Katie looked around the cottage and, if she was honest, there weren't many places where you could hide a trapdoor. There wasn't even a concealed cupboard or hidden panel in the wall. The place itself was simply laid out; a kitchen, a small living-room, and that was basically it. There was a threadbare and heavily soiled rug, which she begrudgingly pulled back, revealing a flag-stoned floor. She vigorously rubbed her hands in her clothes to wipe away any loose dirt or, well, she didn't want to think what that stain was on the rug. Nowhere there, she thought, to hide an entrance, tossing the mat back with distaste. There were no other doors to speak of, only the one leading upstairs. She absent-mindedly scratched her head to the sheer delight of her watcher. Maybe there isn't a cellar, maybe the Voice was mistaken; doubts began to fill Katie's mind, too. She searched for a while longer and came to the conclusion that there actually wasn't a cellar after all – or even a hidden room or concealed passageway.

'All right, Kevin, you win. There isn't a trapdoor.' She couldn't be bothered to banter with him any more.

'What now?' Kevin asked. 'This has been a total waste of time,' he moaned.

'I don't know,' Katie replied. 'But for god's sake, be a bit more positive, Kevin.' She cursed and turned to her animal friend. But he wasn't there! 'Monkey, where are you?' Her stomach suddenly tightened with a sinister grip of fear. They'd been so intent on finding the mysterious doorway and bickering with each other that he'd slipped out unnoticed somehow.

'Kevin, quickly, we have to find him,' she said, but then . . .

'Katie, Kevin, come out here.' Monkey's muffled voice seemed to emit from the back of the house. They ran outside in a bid to see what all the fuss was about. Once there, the two teenagers looked at Monkey in disbelief. He was standing at the corner of the cottage by an overgrown hedge, pointing towards it!

'What, Monkey . . . you're going to do a spot of gardening now, are you?' Kevin said flippantly. Katie shook her head.

'Are you going to act this stupid all day? Give him a chance, will you?' Katie exploded, disgusted with his continuing attitude.

'Well, what are we supposed to be looking at?' He stood with his hands out as if giving something away as a gift.

'It's here, smart Alec, the entrance is right here.' Katie was a little puzzled. So was Kevin as they stared at the badly neglected hedge. There was, however, a small section which appeared as a hole in the foliage. On closer inspection, though, Monkey eased back the mass of greenery to reveal . . . a hidden entrance.

'Wow, Monkey, I'm really sorry, you were right. I'm also really impressed.' Kevin apologised. 'I'm sorry, Katie, I get a little worked up sometimes, you know?' Katie just grinned. 'You run hot and cold, Kev.' Kevin moved quickly, and again used the same technique as he'd used opening Mad Maisey's front door – only this time he had to crouch down to get any weight behind it. He pushed his shoulder against the small oak doorway, but it didn't move this time. It was stuck solid! Not to be outdone he tried again, with the same result.

'Hold on, Kev, look . . . there's a handle.' Sure enough, as Katie had said, there was a ring halfway down the panel. Stubbornly, Kevin eased back and jerked hard against the door one more time, not listening to Katie's plea. He hit it with such a pressure that it made a 'dumpth'-like sound! He rebounded off the door and landed with a thud on his backside, right next to Monkey. The impact knocked the wind out of him. Monkey couldn't suppress his laughter and gave Kevin a sly wink so Kevin would bite back. Kevin's expression was of great surprise at first and then it turned to thunder. He was just about to explode in a damning rage when . . . Katie grasped the ring, pondered a moment, then twisted it anti-clockwise and simply pulled! The door opened immediately, but outward rather than inward! That was obviously the way that Kevin thought it was supposed to go. Katie dropped the ring and turned to her companions, looking rather smug. Kevin's face was a picture of embarrassment and it didn't help that Monkey was doubled up in fits of hysterics. Kevin's refrain quickly changed from wild temper to sheepish admiration, and a smile curled his mouth.

'All right, I'll admit it, I do jump the gun sometimes,' he said with a giggle. 'But that's just me I suppose,' he admitted.

'Monkey!' Katie said abruptly, 'That's enough.' Monkey gathered himself together and stopped his fits of laughter. He looked at Katie with a cheeky grin and she glared back. He could see she meant business and he sheepishly bowed his head.

'We're here to do a job. Let's get on with it, shall we?' she retorted. 'Wow, what is that smell?' she said and put her hands over her mouth.

'It's coming from in here, but I can't see anything. I can barely see past the entrance.' Kevin's voice echoed as he peered into the lightless void. His two companions gingerly entered by his side.

'God, it stinks,' Katie said, her face creased up as if she'd chewed a lemon.

'Oh, Yuk! We'll need a lamp or some kind of light, because I'm not going any further without one,' she said, and almost retched; knowing that once they'd got hold of a light, then the next move was to actually go further in.

'I think I saw one in the cottage,' Monkey uttered, whilst scratching the side of his head. 'I'm going back to find it,' he said bravely.

'Monkey, are you sure? I could come with you, you know,' Katie said in support – and to get away from the stench.

'No, it's OK, Katie; I have to do this on my own.' He was adamant.

'I wonder what's in here,' Kevin said, sounding intrigued, excited even. 'I like a challenge.'

'Well, you can lead then and we'll follow you,' Katie replied, hoping he'd agree, but also *knowing* he would, anyway. It wasn't long before Monkey returned with a fully-filled oil lamp and a box of matches.

'Well done, Monkey,' Kevin complimented.

'Yeah, well done.' Katie was underwhelmed, pleased for Monkey finding the lamp, but terrified at what lay ahead. Kevin removed the glass top and struck the match – it lit instantly. He then replaced the glass cover and adjusted the wick and held it up. They were perched at the entrance and as Kevin leant forward, the light revealed exactly what they were up against.

'Wow, look guys!' he said in awe. They were standing at the top of a huge stone staircase. The lamp only exposed the first few metres.

'I've got a bad feeling again,' Katie said with a tremble. 'What *is* this place?'

'I know what you mean,' Monkey agreed. 'I didn't know anything of this.'

'Well, come on, we're here now,' Kevin said bravely and took the first step down. Reluctantly, the others followed.

Chapter 10

A step into the unknown

'This looks as if it goes on for ever,' Kevin's voice echoed loudly.

'Kevin, keep it down, will you? We don't know what's down there.' Katie hissed and cringed at the same time. 'It looks really spooky and we don't want anyone or anything knowing we're here, do we?' she retorted. The deep, blinding blackness and thick, damp odour reminded her of a pit. Not any pit, but one she'd fallen into the last time she was in Reflections. That was frightening to her then, but this place was much, much bigger and scarier. Kevin extended the lamp out as far as his arm would allow. The yellow beam revealed more and more steps.

'Where do these end?' he mumbled to no one in particular. 'The bottom can't be far away now,' he said a little louder, trying to build morale.

The decay that hung in the air made Katie almost gag. She put her hand over her mouth and nose to try and filter out the stench. But it was no use, so she and Monkey followed loyally in Kevin's footsteps in silence. They found the stone steps were easily wide enough for all of them to walk three abreast. Monkey and Katie kept a link with each other by tightly holding hands. But it was starting to get too much for Katie. There was a real fear building up inside her.

'Yuk, it stinks in here, it's stale and damp and horrible.' She retched, but her voice carried and rebounded around the roof of the cave.

'This place has been sealed for a very long time. I can understand it. I mean who would want to come down here anyway? Even if I'd known it existed before, I wouldn't have bothered,' he said to Katie, with a chuckle to try and lighten the situation, but that didn't do the trick either.

She tried to make sense of her surroundings, but there was nothing to focus on except the stone steps that seemed to be multiplying by the second. It got colder, too, the further down they went, and all three shuddered.

'God, it's freezing down here,' Katie uttered, as a fog cloud emitted from her mouth when she spoke. Their footsteps scratched on the surface of the stone, making it sound as if there were an army of them.

'Well, there can't be anyone in the immediate area or they would have heard us by now,' Monkey said in passing.

Down and down they went as if this new world was only made of steps.

'H-how many bloody s-steps are there?' Katie said with a chatter as the ice-cold air made her mouth ache.

'Look, keep going, the bottom can't be far away now. It only seems far because we can't see the end. If this was a fact-finding mission in broad daylight, then these steps would probably feel like nothing,' Kevin assured everyone. They continued, and as they did, something caught their attention.

'What's that noise, Monkey?' Katie asked.

'What noise, Katie? It's so loud with our footsteps

that I can't make out anything else.' Monkey was puzzled.

'It's kind of hissy and squelchy,' she said, more intrigued by the minute.

'Ah, there, look, there's the bottom.' Kevin announced proudly. 'I found it.'

'Kevin, Monkey, stop. STOP!' Katie said with urgency.

'What . . .?' Kevin grunted as he brought the lamp to Katie's contorted face.

'Just shut up a minute. Listen!' Doing as he was told for once, Kevin *did* shut up and Monkey went along with the charade.

'What are you on about?' Kevin asked again.

'Just listen . . . listen.' There was nothing now; no footsteps or heavy breathing, only the hiss and crackle of the oil lamp and something else.

'What is that?' Kevin was straining his ears. The sound could only be described as the worst sound of slurping, sucking and squelching that they had ever heard before.

'It's coming from down there.' Kevin wielded the lamp towards Monkey, who was pointing downwards. He then curiously lifted it so the light shone over the sound.

'Kev, Kevin, why is the floor moving?' Katie asked, with deeply nervous curiosity. For once, he was without a clue.

'I-I don't know,' he stammered, scratching his head and raking his fingers through his scalp. 'Maybe it's a trick of the light? I mean the floor can't really be moving, can it? What other explanation is there?' he asked honestly. 'Can *you* explain it, Monkey?'

'I can . . .' Monkey conveyed ominously. 'The floor isn't moving at all. Look closer.'

'Come on, Monkey, don't keep us in suspense. What is it? I'm sure that smell is even worse down here.' Katie asked impatiently.

'It's insects; lots of insects and *they* are moving,' he explained ominously. Kevin squinted as he dropped the lamp to a lower angle and shuddered.

'Oh, crap,' he uttered with a gulp and needlessly started to scratch his arm.

'Oh no, no, no, this can't be happening. No, I can't. I just can't. Let's go back, let's go back right now.' Katie was rambling now and her voice pitch was getting higher and she almost screamed. 'There are millions of them, look, a bloody sea of in-.' She couldn't bring herself to speak any more. Kevin moved even closer and confirmed their fears. Katie wasn't wrong – there were what seemed like millions of the squirming devils. There were beetles in many colours; black, red, green and brown. There were also centipedes, spiders and snakes and a whole host of other creepy-crawlies.

'I can't walk on that lot – there must be another way.' She looked at Kevin and began involuntarily scratching her arm. He held the lamp to her face and could see the fear in her tear-stained eyes. Monkey didn't say a word, but his eyes, too, were as big as saucers.

'What do we do, Kev?' she said with a tremble. 'Go back. Find another way?'

'I'm not going back now, Katie. We don't know if Shelley is down here or not, but if she is, then she might be in immediate danger. The longer we take,' he paused, 'I don't even want to think about it. It took us long enough to get down here anyway. Doubling back to find another way will take us ages – if there is another way.'

'I understand that, Kev, but how are we going to get across this lot. I've only got shoes on, you have boots. I'm terrified of these things. I don't think I can do it. I honestly don't,' she said with a shudder that rippled through her whole body.

'I haven't got boots or shoes,' Monkey said woefully. 'So I'm worse off than all of you.'

'But, Monkey, you must be used to these insects, especially being from the jungle' Kevin said, not understanding the plight of their domesticated friend.

'I haven't mixed with insects in the jungle since I was a baby,' he said with a nervous twitch. 'I live in the world of humans, as you know. I live the same as you and Katie and these creatures scare me as much as they scare you.'

'Which brings us back to the same question, what are we going to do?' Katie continued. 'There's literally no way across.' Kevin didn't answer. He moved the lamp from the three of them and over to the glistening, squirming river.

'Run . . .' he said simply. Katie looked at Monkey. Monkey looked at Katie and they both looked at Kevin with doubt and horror on their faces.

'Run; what do you mean run?' Monkey chirped in. 'I don't understand.'

'Just what I said; run. Run for all we are worth, until there aren't any insects left in our way.' He said it as if he meant it. There was silence from everyone at that point, except the endless crunching, squirming, squelching and clicking of the insect hordes. Katie began to shake violently with cold and fear.

'I-I-I can't. I-I can't do this,' she stuttered, but Kevin was already preparing himself for the sprint. 'Don't do this, Kevin,' Katie said, raising her voice to a higher pitch to counteract the awful sound in the background. 'Please stop . . .' But it was too late. The next instant, Kevin was off like a shot. All at once, Katie realised what was really happening. Kevin held the oil lamp that was now fast disappearing in the distance.

'Monkey, come on, we're losing him!' she screamed. She suddenly burst into a sprint herself, closely followed by a very scared Monkey. Kevin was already way ahead of the two of them. All Katie could see now was the dancing beam of the lamp, getting smaller and smaller.

The light got dimmer and then vanished completely! Her heart was pounding hard and heavy as she made first contact with the creatures. Underfoot could only be described as disgusting, horrible and slimy. With every impact of her foot came the most gut-wrenching sounds, but Katie dared not look down. Monkey, on the other hand, found luck in the shape of creeping vines. They clung to the walls and ceiling of what must have been a passageway of sorts. They made a great climbing frame that he easily shimmied along; he felt as though he was in the jungle again. He came level with Katie and overtook her, but with both of them in darkness, he didn't realise she was underneath him.

Kevin was getting further and further away and not worrying about his two companions. Katie felt distinctly alone, with every thud she whimpered, but didn't stop! She knew that if she did . . . no, she couldn't even think about that.

'Come on, come on, don't stop!' Kevin's faint voice echoed from ahead. Even though she was running for all she was worth, she could feel movement clawing up her legs. The level of insects was quite deep and sucked at every footfall like mud on a boggy football pitch. She pushed on, her body weight making her dig deeper into the soft ground as she ran. Her heart and lungs felt as though they would explode at any second. Her breathing was as rapid as machine-gun fire, and sweat poured down her contorted face. The sounds and damp, putrid odour combined, made her heave to the point of gagging. The creatures were edging up her legs – she could feel them! She took a heavy breath, but the constant gagging and gurgling in her throat erupted into a full vomiting frenzy. She lost her rhythm and grabbed her stomach as she spewed. With all this going on, she inevitably overbalanced and fell headlong into the greasy, wriggling world of insects! Katie landed with a shloop. Her whole body became alive with what seemed like a million tiny terrors. Climbing, crawling, and scurrying into her hair, ears and inside her clothes. She tried to scream, but her mouth only gave the insects another avenue of attack! She had to get out and frantically pulled up and lifted herself to her knees. Then in a wild frenzy of panic she spat, chopped, slapped and generally tried to fend off everything in one go. Try as she might, the more she fought the creatures, the more they came!

'GET OFF ME . . . YOU VILE CREATURES.' she screamed in a wild frenzy.

In the midst of her Kung Fu extravaganza, she noticed a light in her pocket and quickly retrieved the stone. An instant effect took place! The strong beam from the jewel beat off the onslaught of the insect war. In the time it took the creatures to cover her body, they all disappeared! In one swoop, everything retreated and left her kneeling in an empty passage.

She stood up. Still panting heavily and with her body violently trembling from the vomiting experience, she began sobbing and shaking. This, in turn, brought a flood of tears. Tears of relief; tears of emptiness. Footsteps reverberated in the tunnel and with it came light as Kevin approached.

'Are you all right?' he said and knelt by her side.

'Y-You l-left me an-d we-nt on t-to s-ave your own sk-in. You left me, you left me, you left me.' she screamed, her voice building and trembling into a crescendo. Monkey got there a moment later and heard her bellowing in full swing.

Kevin went to touch her arm in sympathy, but she snatched it away immediately.

'D-don't t-touch me, Kev-in,'she uttered with venom. 'Don't ever touch me again.'

'Katie, I'm sorry.' He tried to win her with a simple apology.

'I'm also sorry, Katie,' Monkey added. She didn't even lift her head to acknowledge him either. She began to calm as her breathing and heart rate returned to a steady throb. Both Monkey and Kevin felt really bad at leaving her and everything fell silent for a long time.

'OK, I'm ready, let's go!' She burst back into life. 'Let's move on, *together,* shall we?' she said getting to her feet after placing the stone back in her pocket, and off she went. Her two companions shuffled along behind and drew level. Monkey reached for her hand and she reluctantly closed her hand around his.

Chapter 11

A dead end

They had been walking the long, quiet corridor for what seemed like hours, without speaking to one another. The only sounds besides their echoed footsteps and sharp breathing was the drip, drip, drip of trickling water and the scurrying of rodents. This put Katie on edge, especially after her insect ordeal. The ground beneath their feet was slippery and damp and every now and again they would splash through a puddle. The walls and ceiling were covered in a green slime that glistened with the light from the lamp and then faded into black. It did curiously become warmer, too, the deeper they penetrated the unchartered mine.

'Monkey, have you any idea where we are in Reflections?' Katie spoke up.

'I don't know, Katie. For one thing, I don't know what direction we're walking in and how far from the surface we are either. I mean this place is amazing. All the time we've been above not knowing that there was this tunnel below,' he said, feeling totally overwhelmed.

'Hey, shush, you two, I can't concentrate.' Kevin rasped. 'We need to find out where Shelley is down here.'

'We know, Kev. But trying to do this on your own, without our help, is not going to make things any easier,' Katie said and stopped abruptly. 'Kevin, stop!' She uttered ominously.

'What now? What's the matter?' he said in surprise.

'What is it, Katie?' Monkey asked.

'Look, shine the lamp here,' she said pointing.

'Huh, where? Katie, what is it I'm actually looking for?' he asked, but did as he was told.

'Kev, do you have to question everything?' Monkey asked begrudgingly. Kevin tutted and mumbled something before he saw the indent in the wall that Katie was so excited about. This caught his full attention and he leaned closer and held the beam more steadily. There was a dished insert that could easily have been a natural water basin. The water inside looked crystal clear and Katie was dry mouthed. She cupped her hands together and scooped the liquid to her mouth. Kevin smacked his parched lips together and swallowed.

'Careful, Katie, it could be, you know, poisoned,' Monkey warned. Kevin and Monkey looked on as she ignored them and hungrily swallowed. Then she took a second scoop and a third. They both looked on and were mimicking her swallowing. She stepped aside and took the lamp from Kevin's willing hand.

'Go on, it's delicious.' He dove straight in and lapped it up as if it was going out of style.

'Oh, this is wonderful. It's cool and refreshing and . . . and,' he took another big gulp. When he'd finished, Monkey took his turn until they were all satisfied.

'Definitely the best observation you've had today,' Kevin smiled. They'd truly forgotten, in all the excitement, to bring a container with them. Kevin secretly cursed himself. He had been on many a hunting or fishing trip and always kept water with him. Why hadn't he done so this time? He had to keep his wits about him, he scolded himself.

'Well, if we can't find any water further down, at least we know there's plenty here,' Monkey conveyed.

Kevin retrieved the lamp from Katie and continued walking, but it wasn't long before they came to an abrupt stop again!

'Grrr, I don't believe it,' he spouted angrily. 'That's *all* we need.'

'What's the problem?' Monkey asked, as he poked his head around Kevin's leg.

'A fork.' Katie hissed when she saw it. 'A fork,' she repeated. 'What do we do now?'

'There's nothing for it – we're going to have to choose which one to take.' Kevin reasoned.

'We would do better if we split up,' Katie announced.

'Split up, Katie, but how? We have no light,' Monkey stated.

'He's right, Katie, there's no way any of us could stumble around in the dark,' Kevin said. 'Besides, we're stronger in a group. We don't know what is down here either, do we?'

'How are we going to choose then?' Katie asked, and sat on a large rock that looked a little like a stone bench. Monkey sat beside her and Kevin placed the lamp in the middle and rested down on his haunches.

'Mmmm, this is a predicament,' Monkey added. All their faces reflected in the pale glow of the lamp.

'Well, I know what to do,' Kevin said simply. They waited for his suggestion.

'Well, Kevin, are you going to keep us in suspense or tell us this wonderful idea?' she asked.

'You decide which way to go,' he said, as his features contorted in the light of the lamp.

'What do you mean – I have to decide?' she said, sounding a little shocked. 'Why me?'

'Yes, Kevin. Why Katie? Can't I have a say for once?' Monkey countered in reaction.

'No, Monkey.' Monkey looked meek and Kevin continued, 'because a woman's intuition is always supposed to be foolproof. Women apparently always make the right choice – I trust you Kate.' Katie looked positively stunned for a moment.

'All right then, I will choose,' she said adamantly, and stood up and took the lamp at the same time. She walked into the centre of the V and glanced from left to right and back again. She shone the lamp in the left corridor and gently swayed into the right. She admitted to herself that there wasn't much in the way of difference to either side. She took the lamp and repeated once more, but as she did so this time there was a small vibration in her pocket that made her flinch. She brought the lamp back to centre. Once more, she swept to the left and then back to the right. The same thing happened again and that told her the stone wanted her to go right. That must be where Shelley is, she thought.

'Katie, what are you doing, signalling a train.' Kevin griped from behind.

'This way,' she said with certainty and off she went. Her two companions followed like obedient dogs, more surprised than anything. It wasn't long, though, before negativity reigned once again.

'A dead end; well, that's it. That's just great.' Kevin grizzled. Katie winced and clenched her teeth without the others knowing. I made a mistake, she thought, we should have gone the other way. Then another thought struck her. If the other way was a dead end too, then it was back along the tunnel and through the insects. No, she thought, and closed her eyes.

'All this way and a bloody dead end! We should have gone the other way,' Kevin said, cheerful as usual.

'Shhh, Kevin, you gave Katie the choice.' Monkey scolded. Kevin shook his head.

'Could I have the lamp back, please?' he asked. He held it closer to the wall and studied the granite surface. He scoured it, looking for some clue, any clue that may help to get through.

'It can't be. Shelley needs our help – we can't let her down now.' Katie's eyes creased in frustration and two lines of tears escaped the corners.

'I agree, Katie, let's go back and maybe try the other way,' Monkey added. Kevin stared blankly in front of him.

'Hold on, there's something here; it's a small hole and some kind of pattern that's been gouged into the stone,' he mumbled.

'What sort of pattern?' Katie and Monkey expressed in unison.

'I don't know, have a look for yourselves!' he stepped back out of the way and kept the lamp in place, allowing them to see.

'Well, that means that someone lives or lived down here,' Monkey assumed. Katie studied the design. It represented what looked to her like four crescent moons surrounding a circular centre. The moons were close to each other, but didn't actually touch. The shape in the centre was roughly the size of a small pebble. It wasn't completely round and it reminded her of something. She mulled it over and over in her mind and then it dawned on her like an avalanche. She'd been carrying that shape around with her for a solid year; no wonder she recognised it!

'What a fool I am,' she said, shaking her head at being so stupid.

'What, Katie, what do you mean? Say something for goodness sake!' Kevin said, hating being kept in the dark.

'Katie,' Monkey looked at her with wonder. 'What is it?'

'The stone,' she blurted, and dipped her hand into her pocket.

'It can't be that simple, surely. That would be way too much of a coincidence.' Kevin interrupted sceptically.

'The only thing that would prove it, Katie, is to try it,' Monkey said with his eyes wide and a jerky nod. She grasped it and it was still warm. She raised her hand and lined the stone to the diagram. It looked roughly the same shape. She held it there, hovering like a helicopter ready to touch down. What if it fell inside the rock and she lost it forever? She couldn't help Shelley any more. What should she do? Her head was swimming with doubt; should she . . . shouldn't she? She couldn't make any decision until Kevin made up her mind for her.

'Katie,' Kevin barked, making her jerk forward and accidentally push the stone into the hole.

'Kevin, you idiot.' She grappled for it, fumbling and scratching, but it was too late – it had locked into position. She gasped and put her hand to her mouth and held her breath.

They didn't have to wait long for a result, because the stone began to glow and illuminate the four surrounding moons. There was a gush of excitement from all three of them. In unison, the four moons slowly rotated and inside the rock there was clanking and grinding of dry stone. The glowing jewel was bright and Kevin dropped the lamp to his side. Monkey instinctively held on to Katie's hand tightly. They were breathing hard now, but waiting, not knowing what to expect. The intensity of the beam was fast exceeding that of the lamp. There was a rumbling that sent vibrations straight through the tunnel. The wall itself slowly retracted, causing a curtain of dust to hang in the air, but the rich circle of light still cut through. The wall had changed into a solid rock door that slid back about half a metre and stopped! For moments, there was nothing, and a sinking feeling ensued. Again, after a short pause, the rumbling began again. This time it descended into a slot in the floor. Slowly and steadily it sank into the ground like a tombstone being swallowed by the earth itself. Soon the light disappeared as the wall grounded and levelled to the floor surface. Everything went quiet, except for the dry coughing of the three travellers. They looked on in disbelief and did nothing until it began again. There was another cycle to be performed by this magic of mechanics.

This time the wall was rising from the ground and

they realised what they had to do. It was obviously a doorway and once the system began it would open and close automatically. So there was no time to stand still and watch – they had to move, fast!

'Come on, it's closing back up,' Kevin shouted above the roar of the ever rising granite slab. He suddenly remembered the oil lamp and quickly turned and grabbed it. Without saying another word, they rushed forward and jumped over. Monkey didn't jump high enough and fell backwards. Katie and Kevin were through.

'Wow, that was close,' he exclaimed. He put the lamp down with a satisfied sigh. He looked at Katie and she back at him and both smiled as their faces glowed in the bathed light of the oil lamp. Then they realised; Monkey hadn't made it. Katie looked at the fast diminishing gap.

'Monkey, come on!' she screamed and tried to get back over the ascending stone. It was halfway up when Kevin leant over and gripped Monkey's arm. He tried to pull, but as the rock continued to rise it lifted him off his feet. He was balancing precariously like a see-saw and Monkey was not letting go of his hand. Katie had no time to think and pulled with all her strength on Kevin's legs.

'Pull harder, pull harder,' he screamed from the other side, barely getting his words out because his lungs were squeezed of air. Katie gave one last, hard pull and Kevin managed to flip himself back. He pulled Monkey through with him just before the door sealed itself shut! They all collapsed in a tangle of legs and arms as the door eased back to its original position. There was a brief pause until the silence was broken with Katie erupting into a fit of hysterics. Kevin was most put out and Monkey was still coming to terms with getting through unscathed and not being crushed to death.

'What the hell are you laughing about?' Kevin snapped. This only sent Katie into a deeper belly laugh that she found difficult to escape.

'You-you were bent dou-ble . . . kicking your legs like a spider on an energy drink . . .' she exploded. 'And the wa-ll was rising and threatening to . . . cut you in half . . .' She took a breath in between huge bouts of giggling. 'You wouldn't keep your legs still.' She couldn't continue and Monkey, now seeing the funny side, if there was one, broke into laughter, too. Eventually, Kevin began to giggle and finally cracked up, too.

By the time they'd all settled down, Katie, through tear-soaked eyes, noticed the stone jutting out from the wall. It wasn't shining brightly any more, but was more of a dull glow again and it was on their side of the wall.

'Look, Kev, it must have come through like some sort of key.'

'Wow, maybe we can use it again later,' he commented. She got up and picked it out and put it back in her pocket.

'Come on then, you two silly beggars,' Monkey said, as he got to his feet, 'Shelley needs us.'

Chapter 12

Sub Reflections

Kevin picked up the lamp and held it up so he could get a better picture of where they were. The ceiling this side was much lower than the other side of the door. The luminous yellow glow of the oil light threw a wide blanket of soft colour along the corridor. All three peered into the distant tunnel, straining their tired eyes.

How much further, I wonder, Monkey thought, wanting more than anything to see Shelley again soon. How much further, Katie thought, because she wanted to see the open air and get out of this dark, damp world she was now in. Shelley, Shelley, where are you? Kevin called in his head – was he ever going to see her beautiful face again? Dismay and depression seemed to follow them like an uninvited guest.

The tunnel seemed to get narrower as they walked further along and the ceiling definitely got lower. They knew this physically because they had to stoop down in order to move.

'This feels as if it's going to close off completely,' Katie said, as desperation began setting in. 'Maybe you shouldn't have listened to me and gone the other way.' She moaned, 'I knew I'd made a wrong decision.'

'You didn't make a wrong decision Katie; have a little faith in yourself. I don't think this is going to bring us to a dead end at all,' Kevin said with an air of positivity.

'How do you know?' Katie responded.

'Because, well, whoever made these tunnels wouldn't have made a solid rock doorway to hide, well nothing. Would they?' he explained.

'Kevin's right, Katie, it was a huge feat of engineering to move that door. No one would have gone to all that trouble and not have it lead somewhere.' Monkey spoke honestly. The passage got to the point where Kevin and Katie had to bend double. Monkey was fine walking normally, being half their height.

'Oh, my back is killing me,' Kevin groaned, resembling an aged sea captain, bent over with his lamp held aloft.

'Mine too. I'm also fed up with looking at your butt.' Katie joked.

'Oh, ha-ha,' Kevin retorted. 'Do you do magic tricks as well as jokes?'

'Katie, you shouldn't talk about such things', the voice of Monkey squeaked from behind. She grinned.

'You're so old fashioned, Monkey. Lighten up,' she said bluntly.

'Maybe I am but . . .'

'Ssshhh,' Kevin whispered with urgency.

'What is it Kev?' Katie asked.

'There's light,' he said as they emerged from the cramped area of the tunnel and stood up in the open arena that lay before them.

'Oh, I can stretch at last.' Katie lifted both arms upwards and arched her back for a few fleeting moments. 'Oh, this is heaven,' she swooned.

'Ssshhh Katie, there's something there.' Kevin's

voice had an urgent tone about it. It was still pretty dark, but all three could make out an entrance towards the other end. It gave a white, luminous light that cascaded through the silhouette of a figure. It stood rigid at the other entrance of the corridor as if painted on to the brilliant background.

'What is that, Kev?' Katie whispered, as a chill ran through her.

'More to the point, why hasn't it seen us?' Monkey added. 'It just doesn't seem to be moving; very strange.'

'You're right, Monkey,' Kevin said in a hushed tone. 'There are only two sources of light in here, the one behind that creature or whatever it is, and our lamp. I would have thought it could see us quite easily,' Kevin said.

'We have to get closer,' Monkey said.

'I don't like this,' Katie said with trepidation.

'Girls never like anything fun.' Kevin grinned. 'Live a bit and do something dangerous.'

'We should hide,' Katie said, ignoring his suggestion.

'There's no point hiding, Katie. If it was going to attack us, it would have by now,' Monkey said sensibly, weighing up the situation.

'So, what, we walk right up to it?' Katie said flippantly.

'Yeah, pretty much,' Kevin replied.

'I agree,' Monkey responded.

'Are you two nuts?' There was no answer as the two

unlikely comrades started walking towards the apparition.

'Well, I never saw that coming,' Katie mumbled to herself. 'Hey, wait for me.'

All three advanced until they were within three or four metres of the figure.

'I'm afraid, Kevin,' Katie whispered as they stopped. The figure was easily two metres high and broad at the shoulder. It wasn't man or woman, but had a similar frame; two arms, two legs, a torso and a large head. It was dressed in a Roman toga and its whole frame was glistening white. The creature's face was long, with no depiction of a nose or ears. It had two spaces on its face where eyes would normally be found, but the lids were tight shut. Moving down its body, the arms tapered off to hands, but its feet were totally hidden under the drape of white. Kevin put down the lamp and stared.

'What's it doing?' Katie asked in anticipation, looking up at the calm look on its face.

'Nothing,' Monkey spoke up, 'absolutely nothing, very strange. If it's a guard, well it's sleeping.'

'Not much of a guard if it doesn't do anything.' Kevin sounded almost disappointed.

'There's got to be more to this, surely?' Katie was staring at the blank expression on the alien's face.

'Why not try talking to it and asking it if we can pass?' Monkey said sensibly. Kevin and Katie looked at one another and shrugged their shoulders together.

'Ok then,' Kevin spoke up. 'Er, excuse me, but can we pass?' he questioned. There was no movement of expression on the guard's face, or any other movement come to that.

'Please sir, will you allow us to get past?' Katie asked innocently, but there was no reaction.

'Let's just walk past it then.' Kevin said, as his patience got the better of him.

'No, Kev, don't.' But before she could say any more, he did as he usually did and barged through. He only actually got to within two more metres when the ancient guard lifted up its right arm. It must have sent invisible power surges which knocked Kevin completely off his feet and sent him through the air and crashing to the floor. Katie screamed and Monkey raced over to see if he was all right. Katie joined him and they both knelt each side of him. Kevin's eyes were closed and it seemed as if he wasn't breathing.

'Monkey, do something!' she shrieked. 'Come on, Kevin, wake up.'

'Like what? You're the person with medical experience around here. *You* do something.' Monkey squeaked back.

'I'll have to give him mouth-to-mouth,' she said, preparing to hold his nose and part his lips. Kevin burst back into life, his mouth wide open and his chest heaving. Katie and Monkey shot back with a start.

'You're all right, phew,' Katie said with relief.

'Where am I? What happened?' Kevin's eyes were blazing with confusion.

'We're in a cave, Kev. Can't you remember?' Monkey retorted.

Kevin took in his surroundings. 'Oh, yeah, I remember,' he said, building his memory back.

'I told you not to go any further, but you're so bull-headed sometimes.' Katie scolded, like a mother telling off her children for doing wrong. Kevin just looked at her.

'That thing is really powerful,' he said.

'It's got some kind of defence built in and hit you with some force.' Monkey said. 'What did it feel like, Kev?'

'Like being hit with a huge hammer,' he recalled.

'Then how are we supposed to get past it?' Katie stood looking directly at the guard. The guard's hand had returned back to its side whilst they were tending to Kevin. It stood silent and motionless again.

'We have to get past it, Katie. It's the only way to find Shelley,' Kevin said desperately. 'Look, what if I charge it and when it's taking care of me, you two run past it and on through the tunnel.'

'Dumb idea, Kev.' Katie added with a hint of sarcasm, 'Number one, were not leaving without you; number two, what makes you think something that ingenious can't fire at three targets at the same time?' Kevin fell silent and gritted his teeth in anger.

'We have to go back and find another way.' Monkey said.

'We haven't time for that, Monkey. We've wasted enough already,' Katie said and helped Monkey lift Kevin to his feet. He winced at the pain building in his chest.

'That thing must have really given me a belt,' he said as he tried to rub away the pain. They all stood in front of the being, but at a safe enough distance.

'We can't go round it. We can't reason with it; there's only one thing for it.' With a huge surprise to Monkey and Kevin, Katie stepped forward.

'Katie, what are you doing?' Monkey said. Kevin went to stop her by putting a hand on her shoulder, but she pushed him away. She continued and stopped half a step short of Kevin's attempt. She didn't really know what she was doing, but felt a warmth on her leg; the same warmth that she'd felt when she'd encountered the insects – it was the stone. She dipped her hand into her pocket and grasped it. She plucked up courage and took one more step. As she did so, the being began raising its arm in the same fashion as it had on Kevin. Katie, with heart pounding in her chest, whipped out the stone and held it in front of her. It was already glowing and before the creature could fully extend its arm, a strange thing happened. The stone emitted a flash of light that immediately dimmed, and the guard's body pulsed and faded; pulsed and faded, pulsed and faded until it completely disappeared. Instinctively, Katie placed the stone back into her pocket and gasped at her own actions.

'Katie, where did you learn to do that?' Kevin asked smartly.

'Yeah, likewise,' Monkey added.

'I-I don't really know,' she answered in a stutter, because she could hardly believe she'd done it herself.

'The entrance is free to walk through,' she said simply.

'This trip is getting weirder and weirder,' Kevin admitted. Katie smiled in the darkness to herself, chuffed at the power she held in the stone.

'I don't know how you did it and I wish I'd known before I'd attempted my approach, but I guess we can carry on now,' he said, still rubbing his chest.

'Well, there's no time like the present, is there?' Katie said, with an air of confidence. 'Grab that lamp, Kev, and let's see what else is in store for us.' They all walked through the wide cave mouth and on to whatever lay ahead. It seemed darker in this passageway.

'It looked lighter when that guard thing was in front of the entrance,' Katie said.

'Never mind, we still have the lamp,' Kevin said. They continued their journey through the deep cave network and it wasn't long before something else caught their attention.

'What's that? Not *another* monster guard', Katie asked while trying to make out what looked like a square block of luminous light.

'I can feel air, cold air, flowing on my face,' Monkey said with glee.

'No, wait, you're right, Monkey, it actually looks like... daylight! There is a cool breeze too. I can feel it.' Kevin was anxious now.

'But it can't be, can it?' Katie said and craned her neck towards Kevin, who didn't say another word for a moment, then announced . . .

'I think I know what this is,' he spoke, with an air of recognition.

'How on earth could you know what anything is down here, Kev?' she questioned doubtfully. 'I mean, not one of us has ever set foot down here before. We didn't even know this place existed.'

'Kevin, explain!' Monkey cut in, filled with curiosity. 'You *do* look as though you know something. Let us in on the secret.'

'Well, I don't know for sure, but my father *did* tell me once that there was an underside to Reflections. I didn't know if he was just making it up as a bedtime story, but now I'm beginning to wonder if it's true.' He ended his statement without taking his eyes off the block of light.

'Well, a world beneath a world doesn't make much sense, especially if it has a natural light, but there's only one way to find out,' Katie said, frowning. 'Shall we?' She lifted her hand in an invitation.

'Hold on now you two,' Monkey intervened and stopped them in their tracks. He looked worried and even scared.

'What's the matter, Monkey?' Katie asked, her eyes filled with curiosity.

'Look, Shelley has been taken who knows where? Maybe down here, maybe not. Whoever did it wants something from her unless . . .' He stopped, but they could tell there was a lot more spinning around in his head.

'Unless what, Monkey?' Kevin piped up. Monkey looked first at Kevin and then warily at Katie. 'Unless she's already been . . .'

'Stop now, Monkey. We can't even think that way,' Katie expressed, breathing harder with every word as though it hurt her to say it.

'All right, but whatever has happened to her, there's something evil behind it.' He stared with deadly eyes at the pair of them. 'And that evil will be expecting someone to look for her. We must be very careful,' he said in a darkened tone, his black eyes reflecting yellow from the lamp.

'Are we all ready, then, to see what is waiting for us? We've come this far!' Kevin's impatience was obvious. Everyone nodded. 'OK, then.' Without any more interruption, they walked briskly towards their fate. Katie's stomach tightened with every step. As they got closer to the end of the tunnel, the light became brighter and bigger.

'Good grief, it actually feels like we're outside.' She couldn't quite get her head around it. There was a breeze for starters, which made the air colder. Then there was that feeling of actual openness as if they were walking out instead of in. 'How could we be outside? We've been below ground for hours.' Her mind was in a whirlwind of thoughts. She looked at Kevin, who was busy pondering on his own.

'I don't think we'll need this any more,' he said as they approached the end of the passageway. So he blew out the flame and placed it on the floor.

'I think you're right, Kevin,' Monkey said, almost as a squeak, also filled with trepidation. They stopped and gazed – there wasn't a sound from any of them! They stood on the abyss of a new world, it was breathtaking. The end of the passageway was wide – about the size of the double doors to maybe an old library or something. Kevin walked through and still didn't say a word, closely followed by his two companions. Katie unintentionally let out a gasp and quickly put a hand to her mouth! All three also shaded their eyes from the brilliance. It was amazing, like opening Pandora's Box for the first time. Monkey stayed silent in his thoughts. Like the receding curtains of a theatre, Sub Reflections revealed itself. The plinth they were now stood upon was actually a platform that perched at the top of a long, sweeping, cascade of stone steps. But what took the three of them completely by surprise was the enormity of the landscape. It was like looking into a huge box of chocolates. It was definitely a city of some kind, a long-forgotten civilization. Above them was sky! It looked like real sky with grey moving clouds, depressing, overbearing and definitely not summertime. It looked like the real sky above Reflections.

'This can't be true.' Katie had difficulty getting her head around this fascinating new place. Was it always like this, Katie thought? She noticed there wasn't a sun but with the overcast sky it could be hidden. Kevin, too, was looking at the vastness and he brought his gaze lower to the city itself. There were lots and lots of buildings trailing off into the distance – layer upon layer of houses and what looked like official buildings for government people. Everything was speckled around them like sprinkles on a birthday cake. It was all toned in the same colour, like a giant city of sand. It was very drab to say the least.

'What's that?' Monkey broke the silence as he pointed into the backdrop. There were huge columns right at the back which nobody except Monkey had noticed at first. But then, on closer inspection, they stood out as arms inviting newcomers into this strange land.

'This place is really depressing,' Katie uttered. 'I wonder if there's anyone here?'

'What is this place? And is Shelley here?' Kevin said dryly. 'I mean, it's totally deserted. Where is everyone?

A city of this size you'd think there would be somebody here. My father was right after all.'

'These are things we are going to have to find out,' Katie sighed. 'I don't like the vibe it's giving off. It's so . . . I don't know . . . negative.'

'As you just mentioned Kevin, where are all the people? I have so many questions,' Monkey said shaking his head.

'OK, come on, we haven't any more time to lose.' Kevin was already descending the steps. 'If she's here, then we'll find her.'

'Kevin – stay close and wait for us, you know what happened last time. We must all stick together,' Katie insisted. As they shuffled their way downwards, every footstep echoed and called out. Small puffs of dust lifted from the disturbed surface. The air was dry and the atmosphere humid. They approached the bottom and once on ground level, the city looked even more daunting than it did up top. The city itself looked like a maze of sorts, with gaps at every angle.

'What are we looking for?' Katie whispered.

'I don't know,' Kevin snapped back. 'I'm as new here as you are.'

'Kevin, come on, she was only asking,' Monkey said in her defence.

'All right, sorry Katie, I don't know and I don't know what direction to go either,' he admitted before she asked any more awkward questions. 'Hold on.' He turned and retraced his steps halfway up the staircase. He stood there for a moment just looking, sweeping his eyes over the city, from side to side. He then stopped at one particular place.

'What is it, Kevin?' Monkey called out.

'If we head toward those pillars, maybe there's something to help us there.' He looked down at his companions and shrugged his shoulders.

'Agreed,' Katie said simply and looked at Monkey.

'Agreed.' He also relented. Kevin skipped back down and the small dust clouds he was creating were soon whipped up and blown across the city.

'Well, the voice has been right about everything so far. Perhaps it won't be long before we find Shelley.' He winked at Katie and it brought a smile to her pretty face. He was getting closer and it made him feel warm inside. Shelley was the love of his life and he needed to find and rescue her and nothing was going to stop him. He took the lead and the others followed. Katie, though, had a tight knot in her stomach, but kept her thoughts to herself. Monkey followed on aimlessly. He wanted Shelley to be alive as much as anyone. But there was something sinister about this place, something really evil. What it was he wouldn't know until he came into contact with whoever kidnapped her. He took a deep breath, tried to clear his mind and followed his friends closely.

Chapter 13

Sand City

'Which way, Kev?' Katie asked, looking baffled at the many different directions offered to them. He stood looking ahead, and his friends could tell his mind was working overtime.

'Well, the pillars are dead ahead, so I guess that's the way we go.' He gestured there with his hand.

'I *do* wish you wouldn't use that word, Kev.' Katie squirmed.

'Uh...what word? What are you on about?' he said, looking more confused by the second.

'I think she mean's dead, Kevin,' Monkey intervened bluntly.

'It's just this place, it's so...'

'Dead!' Kevin joked with a smirk, before Katie could continue. She glared at him.

'OK, sorry,' he relented. 'Let's go this way, then, straight ahead. Will that do you?' he said and marched on with purpose. He chose a narrow street which was the more obvious and direct route, he presumed. The street itself was only wide enough to take two people abreast, so Kevin, as usual, took the lead and Monkey and Katie walked side by side behind. Everything was covered in sand as if the sand man himself had come and coated every scrap of ground. Each house had a hole for a window with no glass to stop the elements, only wooden shutters and little wooden doors.

'With all this sand blowing about, it must get into

everything. Those shutters will only keep out *so* much grit,' Katie surmised. 'It's so dry here, how could anyone survive?' They continued walking and observing. Some doors were open and some weren't, but as they quietly investigated each random house, none of them contained people, animals, nothing. No one came out to greet them or shun them. Except for the wisps of sand being tossed around in the breeze, there was only quiet to greet them. A sinister, hollow quiet, one you didn't want to be left alone in.

'Monkey, this place is really spooky,' Katie said, looking deeply into his eyes. 'If Shelley is here, what has happened to her, I wonder?' A shiver reverberated down the length of her back and made her shudder.

'Think positively Katie, we don't need a negative attitude now. There's enough negativity here to last a lifetime,' Monkey said. He was completely right, she thought. They proceeded further, but something was puzzling Katie, then she realised. She swept her gaze down to the ground and from side to side.

'Monkey, have you noticed something?' Katie went to carry on.

'What, Katie?' He answered quickly, still darting his eyes in every which way.

'There aren't any footsteps,' she reported. Monkey instinctively looked down and she was right. There wasn't a single impression anywhere.

'I see what you are saying Katie, but then again the gusting winds would have blown all evidence of footprints away. Wouldn't it?' he concluded.

'I know that, Monkey, but the winds wouldn't have blown *all* the footsteps away, surely. There would have been some left somewhere,' she presumed. 'Look!' She stopped by one house and stood on to tip toes and peered inside. 'There aren't any footsteps inside this house either.' Monkey joined her and climbed onto the sill and he, also, looked inside. It was a dim, soulless place that looked as though it hadn't been inhabited for quite a while.

'You're right, Katie, there isn't any footsteps or much evidence of people being in here for years. This is really starting to worry me.'

'Why?' Katie enquired.

'Well, if there isn't evidence of activity here, then, are we totally in the wrong place?' he concluded.

'We have to believe she is here, I suppose,' Katie said. He nodded and the pair stepped back and continued on their way. At the end of every set of ten houses there were crossroads. These gave way to more of the bland-looking streets going in opposite directions and that gave way to more boring, uninhabited buildings all around.

'Good grief, there must have been a population here at some point, but where are they all?' Katie questioned with impatience. 'There must have been thousands of people.'

'Never mind the population, Katie, where's Kevin?' Monkey asked, looking blankly up the trail. They moved more quickly in order to catch up with him, but to no avail.

'That's *all* we need.' Katie winced. 'Things are bad enough without losing one of our own.'

'Where is he?' Monkey said urgently. 'Doesn't that

boy ever look behind? Always thinking of himself.'

'He could be absolutely anywhere.' Katie said reluctantly.

'I'm here.' A voice came from above. They both looked up to see him sitting on a ledge of a rather large building. 'Are you two going to keep up or what?' he snarled.

'Well, if you didn't go barging off as you normally do, then maybe we wouldn't have to struggle to find you.'

'Haven't you noticed this place is empty of people, Kev?' Katie cut in before they got into a full-blown fight. 'There aren't any people, animals, birds or anything – only us. Don't you find that strange?'

'Yes, of course I do, but we've got to find Shelley and that's all I'm concerned about at the moment.'

'Can you see anything from there, Kevin?' Monkey called out.

'Yeah, we're heading in the right direction,' he answered, and in no time at all climbed down to street level. 'So are you coming?' he said, and forged on. They instinctively followed. After a while, he tilted back his head and looked directly at the sky. The clouds were fusing and overlapping into dark, ugly masses, leaving huge black shadows on the landscape. I should have brought the lamp, he cursed to himself. He came to a dead stop and his two companions nearly walked into him.

'What's the matter?' Katie uttered in surprise.

'Look, it forks in different directions. I'm not sure which one to take,' he answered honestly.

'Which way do you think, Kevin?' Katie asked.

'Well, I would say right and see where that takes us,' he remarked, and moved on.

'I don't like the look of that sky,' Monkey said solemnly.

'Yeah, I know what you mean,' Katie responded. 'We're in for a storm.'

They'd got to a section of the city with a gentle, upward climb which took them to a flatter area. The houses broke away to make a path to bigger, more important-looking buildings.

'We're at the business end of the city by the look of things,' Katie surmised. These weren't only taller than the rest, but also grander in stature. One resembled a type of church, with a weird-looking steeple that was much the worse for wear. Not the kind of church from where I live, Katie thought. It also had sand-dusted gardens surrounding it. Next was a large, ancient office building, like maybe a town hall. It looked important, like a place that meetings would have taken place; a place for decision making and where rulings might have been passed. Set in between the church and the town hall were a tall set of gates.

'This place is amazing.' Kevin gushed, and stood in awe. The others, too, were suitably impressed with the architecture. Kevin walked a little further and stood before the giant iron gates. It wasn't the gates themselves that left Kevin glued to the spot, but beyond.

'Wow, look at this guys!' he gushed. Katie and Monkey made their way to his side and then realised the main reason why Kevin was so bowled over.

'Oh my,' Katie gulped. Monkey's mouth was so wide he could have caught a large blackbird in it. Kevin remembered the small pillars he saw from the plinth on the city steps. But they were behind the city then from his vantage point. Now he could see that the pillars were far away from the city itself. In actual fact, here and now, what he didn't see was the long, narrow bridge that connected the two. It was dusted in the same colour as everything else and also stretched about a mile long. The three of them slipped through the gap in the gate to get a better look and wished they hadn't. The width of the footpath was a metre or so, but the drop was far more breathtaking and devastatingly scary. Kevin shuffled to the edge and looked down; a hot and cold feeling grated its way through his body. He felt himself breathe harder and a nervous, sickly tremble surged from his stomach.

'Wow!' was the only word he could muster. He felt his knees weaken, he totally didn't like heights. In fact, he would rather walk around and take days rather than go straight across. But to add insult to injury, there was nowhere to walk around. To the left and back to the right was cliff edge and nothing more. Another shudder gripped him and he stepped back half a step.

'Are you really thinking of going across that?' Katie looked at him and knew the answer before he uttered a word.

'Oh, good grief,' Monkey moaned. Kevin, silent in his thoughts, had never seen anything as deep as this in his whole life. When he was a child, his father took him to the sewage plant in which he had created and worked. It was set deep into the Reflections underground. His father showed him around and where they stood was pretty high up, but there were safety rails and platforms to keep him safe. This had no safety rails or rope or anything of comfort, just an open, narrow length of pathway and a long, long drop to the bottom. It made the waterfall where he rescued Katie and Monkey look like a babbling brook in comparison. Katie manoeuvred to one side of him and Monkey edged to the other.

'Wow, Kev. . .' Katie marvelled, but on closer inspection it looked even worse.

'Same here,' Monkey agreed. 'This place is absolutely amazing.'

'Kevin, what is that moving down there?' she said with curiosity and leaned over to take a closer look.

'Get back, Katie, are you mad?' he screeched in reaction.

'Kevin, you're trembling,' she said, feeling his arm and for the first time recognising his predicament.

'You're afraid of heights,' she announced and blinked in astonishment.

'It-It's cold, that's all,' he remarked and snatched his arm away.

'All right, no need to be so defensive. It's OK to be scared, Kev, it's a long way down.

Why, though, is it moving down there?' She repeated her question.

'I don't know, Katie. I can't really make it out,' Monkey said, squeezing his eyes. Kevin, not to appear scared, gently looked down and studied and snapped back. He swallowed hard and panted.

'It-It's a river,' he answered.

'Jesus, that must be a long way down, then, if I couldn't make *that* out,' Katie gushed, not realising she wasn't making things any easier for Kevin.

'Are we going over?' Monkey asked.

'I don't think it's a good idea.' The very words struck fear into Kevin's body, like a sword. 'I-I don't think I can,' he stuttered, still trembling.

'I totally understand you're scared. It's way too dangerous. *Way* too dangerous, but...' she repeated and faded. 'We have to. Maybe you should stay here, though, Kev.'

'Look, I'm not scared, all right, it's just a little chilly,' he barked back, gritting his teeth in embarrassment. 'I just need a little time, that's all – you know, to get my head around it! We've come across a lot today and my head is swimming.'

'Kevin, look, we *have* to do this. Shelley could be over there, you know that!' Monkey cut in. For the first time since leading this expedition, Kevin felt like a weakling. Kevin didn't answer.

'No, Monkey, it's too dangerous,' Katie relented. 'If Kevin can't do it, then we'll have to find another way,' she said with a wink.

'Katie, we have to.' Monkey looked deeply into her eyes. 'You know we have to.' He played along brilliantly. Kevin hated himself and if he could run away anywhere he would have, but for Shelley he knew he had to try! I can do this, he told himself. Katie thought she had done enough to get him on track. Monkey then gave it a go.

'Kevin, we will help you,' Monkey assured him. 'Remember the cottage and the cage? It took a lot of courage for me to go back into that house, but I did, for Shelley. There's no shame in feeling afraid. We've all been there.' He continued as Kevin gazed downward, not doing or saying anything. 'I went back into the witch's house, too, didn't I, when we needed the oil lamp? Katie said she would go because she knew how frightened I was, but I wanted to go back in because of Shelley and to help myself. You can do this Kevin because of Shelley, because you care so much about her. Look, we are here to help you.' Kevin's eyes began to glaze and everyone realised how truly scary this was for him. He was the leader. He was the strong one, but now he needed help and he hated the thought of it. He dried his tears and forced himself to overcome this obstacle. He closed his eyes tightly and bit his lip, willing himself on. With a blink, he opened them again. His mouth opened to speak.

'Let's go before I change my mind,' he said, with grit and determination. Both Katie and Monkey breathed a huge breath of achievement.

'I'll go in front,' Monkey said. 'Kevin, you go in the middle and Katie, you stay at the back. Kevin, whatever you do...'

'I know, I know; don't look down, I've heard it a million times in my life,' Kevin quietly cut in. This was very strange for him, he was the leader. He always led, but this time he couldn't. He was vulnerable and knew for the first time what friends Katie and Monkey were to him. He hated being vulnerable, but glad he had friends to support him.

They began the slow walk across the abyss. The wind was picking up and seemed to be throwing huge handfuls of sand grains into their eyes. It howled in laughter like a raging monster and made it difficult to hear. It felt like the devil himself was taunting them. Every now and then, stones would loosen and fall into the deep basin and crack hard against the sides on the way down, echoing their demise until the sound diminished. It was such a long way down that even the splash of stone hitting the river's surface couldn't be heard. They all had to use their hands at times to wipe the grit out of their eyes. Kevin bent his head forward and squeezed his eyes shut to block out the pain and everything else. But he strayed a little to one side and overbalanced. Katie wiped her eyes and saw him almost step off the end. She screamed out, 'Kevin, stop!'

Her heart almost leapt into her mouth and she reached out and grabbed him before he took the last step to his death. She grabbed him and, as he realised, pulled back. They both wobbled and then steadied themselves back into the centre of the bridge.

'Phew, that was close.' Katie puffed and gazed into his eyes. He seemed to say thank you back without actually saying anything. Monkey was oblivious to it all and carried on. They were halfway along and Monkey noticed that the path narrowed even more for a few metres and then widened again. That's going to be a problem, he thought.

'Kevin, Katie, take it easy here – it's not so wide, but only for a little bit.' Katie looked around Kevin and saw it was only half a metre across.

'Kevin, don't look down. I'll put my hands on both sides of your hips and steady you through. You'll be all right, I promise,' she said calmly, but felt a terrible fear inside. She grabbed him and he took only two steps and the next step his right foot missed the path and slipped off and he came crashing down onto his stomach. Katie let out a scream and fell on top of him, but tumbled over and fell off completely! She still had hold of his shirt with one hand and was dangling precariously in the wind, like a pendulum. She was screaming and swaying back and forth. Monkey turned in horror and tried to grab her, but couldn't reach.

'Katie, Katie, hold on,' he screeched, but Kevin's shirt began to rip under the intense pressure of Katie's whole body weight.

'I'm falling, aaaargh. I'm falling!' she repeated. Kevin immediately thrust out his left arm and gripped Katie by her collar, she stopped falling, but Kevin began slipping over.

'Monkey, Monkey, hold me, bloody hold me!' he bellowed. Monkey grabbed Kevin with both arms as instructed, but he just wasn't strong enough. Katie was still screaming below, but when Kevin looked over to see her predicament . . . he froze! The sheer drop down to the base below was overwhelming. He was losing concentration now with all this inside his head and Katie was pulling him harder.

'Kevin . . . you've got to pull her up.' Monkey was screaming into his ear and the insistent squealing jolted him back into reality. He blinked his eyes and pushed his left leg diagonally. He felt the other edge of the path and hooked his instep onto it and held fast. Katie's grip on his shirt was almost gone and he felt her collar ripping apart under the intense gravity. With one huge hoist he summoned up strength and whipped her up over his shoulder and onto his back! Where he got the strength from he would never understand for the rest of his days, but it worked. Katie clambered off his back and they shuffled along to a wider section. All three of them lay back panting. Katie was the first one to speak and broke the silence.

'You've ruined my blouse, do you know that?' Both Kevin and Monkey burst out laughing. Kevin stood up and shook his head.

'You're mad,' he commented and for the first time in ages his face lit into a warm smile.

'Never mind that, let's get off this flaming bridge.' Monkey mumbled getting back to his feet.

'I second that,' Katie agreed and was helped up by the two of them.

'You OK to carry on, Kev? Are you sure?' she asked and he nodded. 'Thanks,' she said with a wink, 'for saving me.' He just wobbled his head like a nodding dog ornament. The rest of the way over was brisk and they reached the end in record time. Kevin just set his mind on the end and didn't distract from his focus. They didn't need any more excitement and were soon standing at the foot of the great pillars. The pillars themselves were huge and magnificent in stature. Katie thought they looked like the stone columns in Roman times. These were the mighty guards that Kevin had seen from the plinth, but what lay beyond?

Chapter 14

Realm of evil

Katie felt a chill of fear ripple through her body like an earthquake. She stood minuscule against the stone giants that were cold to the touch and the surface itself rough. She craned her neck to take in the full enormity of the columns and stood open-mouthed. She tried to see the peaks, but a threatening, angry sky devoured them in a swirl of grey and black. She almost overbalanced watching the hypnotic, gentle movement of the cloud mass and touched the surface again to steady herself.

'That doesn't look good. It feels as though a storm is coming in, how can that be, we're underground? There should only be a roof of rock above us not this-this internal sky.' She brought her gaze back to earth as the base of her neck began to ache. She rubbed it vigorously to relax the muscle.

'Oh, I don't know, Katie, anything is possible in this world. Strange and wonderful things happened up top, so down here the same things could apply, I suppose. It's crazy but nevertheless, here we are,' Monkey said, peering at the constantly moving sky.

Reluctantly and looking like specks of dust below a giant's legs, Kevin, Katie and Monkey warily pushed on. They moved with trepidation, looking at every shadow and sound, every twitch and hiss. Who knows what hidden dangers they might encounter? Kevin wasn't paying much attention to the others and was looking into the distance.

'This whole landscape is wide open,' he mumbled, 'no cover from attack, nowhere to retreat to when we need to escape.' The survival part of his mind was in full swing. He scanned the immediate area and as far beyond as his vision would allow. This part of Sub Reflections wasn't like the city of sand at all, it was desolate. There were no buildings to speak of but flat, open dusty ground with row upon row of headstones. This was obviously the vast graveyard of the city's occupants. This is the place where all the population were now resting. Sub Reflections, the ghost city!

'This explains what I've been feeling since we entered this world,' Katie said sombrely. 'Death! There's nothing here, Kev, nothing to help us and no one to ask.' She grimaced. 'I feel so useless. We've come all this way and there's no one here. What a waste of time.'

'Yeah, you're right Kate. I don't think she's here either. There's no evidence to suggest she been anywhere near,' Kevin added.

'Oh, I don't like this. I don't like this one bit. Let's go back,' Monkey responded nervously. 'We could find another clue, or search elsewhere; or even go back to the Voice in the Void and ask again.'

'I don't know.' The words were even difficult for Kevin to speak, 'but what if she is here though?' They all looked at one another with shame in their hearts. It was Shelley that they'd gone through all this for in the first place, and now they were thinking of leaving.

'If we feel scared and there are three of us, how do you think Shelley feels?' Kevin added, and he was right.

'We have to go on, no matter what,' Katie said guiltily and was surprised at being the first to announce it. 'I'll admit I am really scared. I've never felt this scared in all my life. We haven't got any backup from the people of Reflections. In a nutshell, we're on our own. But we can't go back, that's not an option.' She was resolute. Kevin nodded towards Monkey and he nodded back in compliance.

'So we continue,' Monkey said, but this time his eyes were brighter and he felt braver somehow. 'Come on then.'

The graveyard was laid out like an impending game of dominoes. One flick and they would all knock against each other and fall flat. Each headstone was bland, in the same dirty sandy colour that the city was bathed in. They were all different shapes and set in rows to the left and right as far as the eye could see. Those they couldn't see were shrouded in the gloom of shadow. There were some that were grander than others. These were set in one corner. One looked a little bit like a miniature version of the White House in the US. Probably someone important, Katie thought. Down the centre was a walkway, it extended into the backdrop and seemed to end at a rock face. There were so many headstones that Katie couldn't comprehend the magnitude of the population.

'What happened to these people, I wonder? I can't understand how they all could have died with no trace of survival, unless it was thousands of years ago.' Katie was thinking aloud. The land was open and the wind forced its way over it. There were no traces of footprints, exactly the same as in the city itself. No one has been here in years, she pondered. Katie stopped when she heard the trickle of running water. This immediately made her thirsty. She smacked her lips and swallowed the imaginary liquid.

'Kevin, Monkey, I'm thirsty – hold on, there's water over there somewhere,' she said dryly. Kevin and Monkey smacked their lips together, too. This land was dry and the dusty wind made the throat burn.

'You've found water?' he said excitedly. He'd been so immersed in his search that he hadn't heard anything; neither had Monkey.

'Where is it, Katie?' Kevin cried.

'Sshh, listen,' she said adamantly. They kept quiet and tried to pinpoint the sound above the rush of the wind. Katie closed her eyes and concentrated.

'It's coming from over here.' She pointed in the direction, still with eyes shut. Immediately to their right stood a kind of cenotaph, which stood above the tombstones but concealed a secret. To their joy, clear, cool water spewed from the mouth of an animal head that was carved into the stone. They all took turns to scoop up water from a dish that caught the spill. Greedily, they slurped and snorted great mouthfuls.

'That doesn't look like any animal that *I've* ever seen,' Katie responded after she'd had her fill.

'Let's hope there's not one still alive down here,' Monkey joked, water dripping from the saturated fur on his chin.

'Come on, we're wasting time.' Kevin interrupted. Monkey looked into the distance.

'Is that an entrance at the end of this graveyard, Kevin?' Monkey asked, his eyes squinting. He was right; at the end of the corridor of tombs there was what looked like a door of some kind. It was so far into the distance, though, and was hard to make out.

'Yeah, it does look like something,' Kevin said, squinting in the same manner.

'Why would Shelley be here, of all places?' Katie questioned aloud this time. 'We are putting a lot of faith in that voice.'

'I don't know, Katie, but it's the only clue we have,' Kevin answered sympathetically.

'There's only one way to find out, isn't there?' Monkey interrupted with a gulp. They all moved further in; the width of the aisle was plenty big enough for at least six of them to have stood abreast. The ground was soft and dusty underfoot, just like the city. Overhead, the clouds grew angrier and the wind was picking up pace.

'This is going to turn into a huge storm by the looks of that sky. We need to find Shelley and get back into the cave and under cover.' Katie said, craning her neck; the sudden rush of dust made her cover her face.

'Let's get inside that shelter, then,' Kevin said in a raised voice to combat the ever-lifting howl of the wind. They walked a while and eventually got to the end. There was a big stone arch that depicted the entrance.

'Is everything big around here?' Katie asked, through the mask of her collar. There must have been doors originally, Kevin supposed. He'd noticed indents each side of the archway that may have supported them. Besides this, and making things a little more intriguing, there was a yellow glow of light coming from the inside.

'There are other people here. There must be, other-wise where's that light coming from?' Monkey piped up. 'Are we going in?' he asked with a tremble. Katie slipped her hand in his and when he looked at her she smiled...a nervous smile.

'We'll never know if we don't,' Kevin added. 'But we must do this very carefully. Look, what if I go in first?' Kevin explained. 'I'm not trying to be a hero or any-thing, honestly.'

'No-no Kev, we do this together.' Katie dropped the cloth from her face and was quick to cut him off.

'But if there's any problem, then I can call out for you two to run and I'll have more chance to get out alone. If there's three of us in there we could all get captured and what help would we be to Shelley?' he reasoned. 'Anyway, if I am trapped then you two can carry on searching, can't you?'

'As much as I hate to admit it, Katie, he's right.' Monkey relented. 'I hate it when you're right,' he quipped.

'No, look, when they split up in the movies, bad things always happen,' she said.

'What are movies?' Kevin looked puzzled.

'Oh, never mind,' she said, remembering that there were no televisions or cinemas in Reflections.

'It *does* make sense though, Katie, for me to go in alone.' Kevin nodded towards her. She eventually nodded back. Kevin didn't waste any time and slipped inside and disappeared.

'Monkey,' Katie looked at him with trepidation and sucked in air through her teeth.

'I know, Katie, but he'll be all right. Give him a little credit,' Monkey answered. Kevin wasn't gone long and soon returned with a look of satisfaction on his face.

'Come on, follow me,' he insisted. They made their way past the main doorway and found they were in an open foyer. The lobby itself was dark and the lighting was coming from further within. Katie paused and Monkey stood firm.

'It's OK, honestly, you can see more further inside,' Kevin assured them, with a look of hope. Monkey and Katie walked on, following their guide, and eventually stepped inside a cavern. A much bigger place than the cave and well ordered. It was vast in size and seemed to have many different doorways at the sides and further back. The ceiling was expertly carved out of pure rock by some skilled craftsman long ago.

'Wow, this place is amazing,' Katie commented in a whisper while gazing every which way.

'There's no one here, you can talk normally, Katie.' Kevin's voice echoed.

'Good grief.' Monkey spoke in a quiet voice, his mind working overtime.

There was a huge slab of stone set to the centre of the room and it was nestled on a plinth. It was partially hollowed into the shape of a throne. There were other smaller slabs of rock set each side of the throne, three of each. These smaller ones were also carved into makeshift chairs. It was obvious that whoever sat in those seats weren't as important as the person who sat on the main stone chair.

'What is this place?' Katie said as the acoustics of the room made her voice echo and amplify.

'Shhh.' Kevin put his finger to his lips, but even his shushing cut through the air like a sabre. 'I thought I heard something,' he said urgently. They stopped talking and listened, but there was nothing. There was, however, the sound of the continuing storm that was lashing the graveyard outside, and the creaks and groans of the inside.

'This must have been an underground civilisation that was here long before the Settlers above ground,' Monkey said. 'They must have ruled Sub Reflections and let the settlers rule above, if they ever knew of above,' he surmised. Katie walked up to the lead stone and gasped in surprise. She examined the surface thoroughly and was further gobsmacked. While the others were occupied, she felt the indentations in the stone. She ran her fingers along the patterns on the backs of the smaller stone seats, too. She then made her way back to the larger throne. The markings were exactly the same as the ones in the tunnel. There was the half-moon pattern that was set in the centre and it was the same shape as her jewel. An excitement gripped her and her stomach tightened at the thought.

'Kevin, Monkey, look!' she called out.

'What is it, Katie. What have you found?' Kevin said, looking intrigued.

'Nobody has been in here for years I don't expect,' she said with confidence. 'I think I've found something that could help us.'

'What is it? What have you found?' Kevin pleaded. 'Come on,' he said impatiently.

'Yeah, what is it Katie?' Monkey was now by her side, too.

'Look at this!' She pointed vigorously towards the design in the rock. 'I'm sure if I put the stone in there it would fit.' She'd already convinced herself.

'It does look the same as the other pattern, and then what?' Kevin asked whilst fingering the hole. 'But we don't know what would happen, Katie. You could start something that we can't stop. This place could be filled with all kinds of traps and mysteries.' Kevin said sensibly.

'Don't do it, Katie. Listen to Kevin for once, he's actually talking sense.' Monkey said with anguish in his eyes. 'We don't know what will happen if you did.'

'Yeah, you're better off leaving it alone, Katie,' Kevin insisted. 'We don't want to seal ourselves in or worse. Let's just find Shelley and get out of here.'

'Katie . . .' The sound seemed to come from everywhere. Katie froze. Monkey and Kevin's eyes were darting everywhere. This alerted all of them!

'That's, that's Shelley. I'm sure of it,' Kevin said, his face filled with hope. 'Shelley, Shelley, where are you?' He began to run around in circles trying to pinpoint the source. 'Keep talking, Shel, and I'll find you.' Kevin was frantically searching, but there was nowhere for anyone to hide. He was feeling the stone walls to see if there was a hidden entrance of some kind.

'Katie.' It sounded again, but it wasn't clear. It came as a sound travelling on the crest of the wind. It dipped and lifted in a swirl around the cavern, all around their heads.

'Shelley, Shelley, where are you?' Katie called. 'Don't go. Please don't go,' she cried.

145

'Shelley, tell us where we can find you?' Monkey joined in. 'Keep talking,' he insisted.

'I'm in a chamber somewhere, but don't come looking for me. He wants the stone. You mustn't let him have it. Go, please go.' She was sobbing now. Katie's eyes filled up, too.

'Ah, Shelley, we can't leave without you. Don't cry, Shel, we will find you.' Katie sobbed.

'Who wants it, Shelley?' Kevin dug in. 'Who wants the stone?' he questioned smartly.

'Davenport,' Shelley answered simply, her voice sweet and light fluttering past their ears.

'Davenport!' Kevin repeated. 'But I thought he went away from this place, never to return.' He felt angry just thinking about him.

(Shelley and Kevin had had dealings with him in the past. Davenport was originally the sidekick of 'Shadrack Scarrat', or 'The Hunter' as he was known before he changed into a good person. Shadrack turned out to be Shelley's father and Davenport didn't like the situation. He then disappeared when Shelley stepped into the frame and was forgotten . . . until now!)

'He killed my father and my grandfather, just to get me.' Her voice wavered, but she carried on. 'He knew that if you found out about me, that somehow you would come and bring the stone. Once he has it, he can rule all of Reflections, above and below.' Her sweet tones were whipping around their heads like a blanket on a clothes line. 'He also has control of the wolves now, too. So you must go and never come back and take the stone with you. You can't help me.' The voice faded and died.

'Shelley . . .' All three of them called, but there simply wasn't any answer.

'Davenport, but how and . . .' The silence didn't last long before the familiar sound of howling wolves filled the chamber.

'Bloody hell, Crusher and Ripper, they're here.' Kevin gulped. 'We have to go, come on, there's no time.'

'But what about Shelley? We can't just leave her here with him and them! I can't leave; I won't leave her' Katie said stubbornly, but she knew the only way to help her friend was not to get caught and figure a way later.

'Katie, at least now we know that Shelley is alive and we have to go and work out a way to free her. But first we must escape the wolves.' Monkey grabbed her arm and they all burst out of the chamber.

Chapter 15

Pursuit

The three friends ran frantically out into the grave-yard, but they weren't expecting what they next encountered! The storm, to their utter dismay, had escalated to enormous proportions. The wind howled through the cemetery, like a vast pack of wolves. In its frenzy, it whipped up dust clouds that blasted out grit, which hurt their eyes and made it difficult to see in any direction.

'Where are we going to go?' Katie screamed through the deafening mayhem. 'It's too far to the bridge and there's no other way out,' she cried, trying to be heard above the wildly hissing wind. 'Oh my god, we'll never outrun the wolves,' she realised. With that still hanging on her tongue, they all heard the echoed and grotesque throaty howling of the deadly hounds. They were closer than ever! The scent of two humans and a chimpanzee was very distinctive and the hunters wouldn't take long to track them down, even in the storm.

'Come on you two, we have no choice.' Kevin screamed out. 'We have to get to the bridge, it's our only hope,' Kevin insisted, trying to focus, 'There is no other escape route.' He cupped his hand over his brow like the peak of a baseball cap, it made no difference. The stinging blanket of sand flicked and slapped at their faces, making it almost impossible to see the road ahead.

'Come on,' Kevin called and they made a break for it across the central pathway, but this left them open and exposed. They hadn't made it halfway along the graveyard before the bone-cracking snarls of Davenport's Razzard wolves burst out of the chamber. This made all three jerk in horror!

'Bloody hell, NOOOO! They're already here,' Katie gasped and felt her heart beat at an even faster rate, she could feel her eyes filling with tears, tears of fear! 'They're here, they're here,' she repeated as she sped behind Kevin and Monkey. 'Don't leave me, please don't leave me behind,' she cried desperately as she tried to keep up. It felt almost the same as being left inside the cave again where the insects were. But this time it wasn't going to be a slow, drawn-out death of insect bites and poison. This time, if she didn't keep up, it would be virtual instantaneous death of being ripped apart; limb from limb in a bloody game of 'tug-o'-war.' With that in mind, she picked up her running pace. They were all at full pelt until a heavy downpour of rain intervened; it lashed down in mighty surges, slowing their progress. Their footsteps were sucked into the ground, draining what strength remained.

'Oh, great, that's all we need,' Kevin mumbled breathlessly, more to himself than anything. The wind had got to blizzard conditions. It was getting more difficult to push against the invisible wall. The ground was becoming slippery and dangerous now, too. Everything seemed to be against the band of three; the elements, the wolves and freedom felt like the last train leaving the station, without them as passengers!

'There it is,' Kevin boomed excitedly through the deluge. They could all just make out the shifting shape of the pillars and the bridge as the dust clouds and downpour distorted their vision.

'I can't hear the wolves. The rain must have slowed them down. Maybe they've lost the scent,' Monkey screeched hopefully.

Panting heavily and gasping for breath, they finally reached the columns. They didn't have time to waste, so as quickly as they could they stepped onto the narrow path that led back to the city. It was going to be even scarier this time and they couldn't dawdle, they had to speed along. There was the wind to contend with, the wolves and the fact that they had to move faster. Kevin tried to glance back, but he couldn't really see anything and if truth be told, he didn't really want to see anything either. All he could actually hear was the violent slash of the wind. But to his horror, he could also hear the not-so-distant sound of the pursuing wolves. A chill ripped through his body, they're closer than he'd thought.

'Come on, let's get onto this bridge. We have to get over to the other side as quickly as we can, or they'll have us,' Kevin called.

'We can't run any more, Kevin, it's too dangerous,' Monkey shouted through the dense mass. 'We have to take our time in case we fall over,' he said gravely. They still couldn't see where they were going and they were reduced to walking in single file, knowing death was only just behind. Kevin didn't think about his fear and took route at the front, then Katie was next and Monkey followed at the rear.

'Hold onto each other's hands. That way, at least, we're linked,' Kevin bellowed. All three groped until they felt each other's grip. This in itself made things feel a little safer. Behind them they could hear Crusher and Ripper and they were at close quarters now!

'Get down on your knees, Katie, and feel your way across,' Kevin shouted out. Katie did immediately as she was asked, it didn't matter to Monkey as he was more natural at it anyway. Kevin could almost feel the wind trying to suck him over the side and down-down-down into oblivion. He stopped! He froze!

'Kevin! What are you doing?' Katie shrieked at high pitch. 'We can't stop now, they're right behind us.' She was crying as she prodded him, but he wasn't moving anywhere.

'Katie, why have we stopped?' Monkey screamed from behind, sounding terrified. 'Tell Kevin he has to move, he has to move quickly. He has to move NOW, Katie.' Monkey was screaming and panicking. Katie crawled along to Kevin's side and within a couple of centimetres of his ear.

'Kevin, listen to me,' she said calmly and at a whisper. 'We need you to be strong now, Monkey and I.' She continued and gently caressed his arm. 'We can't do this without you. If the wolves catch us, you know what they will do. I know you're scared. So am I,' she reiterated. 'You must put your fear behind you and we must go now.' This seemed to bore into Kevin's brain because he twitched and snapped back into his old self. He couldn't actually see over the side as the gusting sand kept stinging his eyes. Soon he was scrambling along the narrow pathway again, trying bravely to ignore his fear. They followed his lead and groped their way blindly along, too. Then they felt the heavy vibration of the dogs bursting onto the bridge. Katie felt her heart lurch in her chest, beating a drum solo. Visibility was virtually at half a metre or so, nothing more.

'Faster-faster,' Monkey exploded, he was screaming.

'I'm trying to, but it's hard in this wind,' Kevin replied in anger. There was suddenly a crack of rifle fire. Katie screamed as a bullet whistled past their ears.

'Come on Kevin. He's a madman. He's trying to kill us.' She frantically pushed at Kevin to move on.

'He can't shoot directly at us in this storm, he may hit his dogs, Katie. We're safe from the bullet, but not the wolves,' Kevin said intelligently.

'You won't get away, stay where you are and I won't let the wolves kill you.' Davenport's voice sliced through the confusion. No one answered his command, they each just carried on scurrying along.

The rock surface was soaked and made it all the more slippery. The sand turned into a slimy paste under his grip. Kevin's hand slid over the edge and he fell flat on his face. Katie felt him lurch forward and quickly grabbed his legs, Monkey bumped directly into her, which almost sent him over the side, too.

'Kevin, are you all right?' Katie cried helplessly.

'Ye-ah, I'm fine-I'm fine,' he said and he pushed himself back up to a kneeling position. 'The path is narrower here, I forgot', he said, as he realised they were only halfway across. Good grief, he thought at that point, we'll never make it. Katie and Monkey took their time as they manoeuvred the thin strip of rock until it became wider again. Suddenly they heard the throaty whimpering of wolves, right behind them, and Katie tensed. Monkey clenched his eyes tight and waited for the attack, but nothing happened!

'What's happening? You useless bloody hounds, get moving.' He heard their whimpers and knew there was something wrong. 'They're right in front of you, I can hear them!' Davenport cursed, not realising that one of his wolves had nearly fallen over the edge at the narrowest point. Crusher was struggling and wouldn't go any further. Ferocious as they were, the thought of falling over slowed them down to a halt.

'You pathetic beasts; kill them. Kill them!' he ranted, but they both remained frozen. 'Get back here.' He bellowed like a mad thing. He had to backtrack to a wider part of the path himself before they could move past him. He gave each one a heavy clout of his fist as they eased by. They yelped in pain!

'You stupid, useless dogs,' he scolded. 'If I need something done, I have to do it myself,' he ranted. Kevin and his companions, while all this was going on, regained composure and shuffled further along the bridge.

'I can't hear them now, Kev.' Katie said excitedly.

'We're not out of the woods yet,' Kevin replied ominously.

'Keep going you two, it's no fun back here you know,' Monkey complained, and with that, Kevin could have screamed for joy because he felt the end of the bridge. He immediately grabbed Katie and touched Monkey on the shoulder.

'Come on,' he whispered. 'We're here.' They scurried up the path. Davenport cracked off another round. It tore into the ground besides them and that gave them the jolt to run even faster.

'Come on, he's closer than I thought,' he said and darted on. The storm was slowing and although still whipping up dust, it was getting easier to see. That's why he's firing with greater accuracy, Kevin thought, but he daren't turn back to find out. The buildings were more prominent and if they could get to them before Davenport caught up there was a slim chance to hide.

'Come on, through here,' Kevin ran ahead with Katie's hand in his and Monkey trailing. They'd gone past the gates and were inside the realm of the city. There were lots of different directions to escape to.

'This way,' Kevin screamed as another bullet swirled past their heads. He took the nearest route and ran through the alleyways. They raced on, weaving their way into the heart of Sand City, hoping to lose their pursuer.

'Go get them, go on,' Davenport snarled at his pets. 'You won't get far!' he bellowed at the city as his voice echoed through the network of streets. Kevin was getting tired and his chest felt tight. Katie felt as though she couldn't run any more, but carried on regardless with Monkey ever faithful at her side. The wind had dropped to a lull and the rain had stopped. This gave the dogs a better chance of tracking and the teenagers a lesser chance of escaping.

'We have to hide somewhere,' Monkey urged. 'Somewhere, soon.'

'Where? The dogs will eventually pick up our scent. We have to keep going.' Kevin panted. 'There's no time. Come on-come on,' he repeated with venom.

'Here, quickly,' Monkey said sharply, pointing to the ground. 'Dive in and roll around. There's no time to explain, just do it,' he ranted excitedly. There was a big puddle of sandy muddied water where the rain had pooled in the street. Katie looked horrified.

'B-b-but I can't, it-it's filthy,' Katie cried, repulsed.

'This is no time to be a little princess, dive in,' Kevin snarled and grabbed her and pushed her straight into the mud. She plunged in head first; but a split second before breaking the surface . . . she saw something glint, a shape! But there was no time to see exactly what it was as she plunged inside the murky world of mud. When she surfaced, Kevin and Monkey were all rolling around getting covered in the thick, stinking compound. They quickly covered themselves until they were almost unrecognisable.

'This will kill our scent, hopefully, anyway,' Monkey said knowingly.

'Let's go over here.' Kevin saw a good place to hide. Katie just followed their lead, still confused as to why she looked and smelled like an old dog. Kevin had found a set of narrow steps that led onto a small patch of ground. They slopped over a wall and squelched out onto a ledge, with only enough room for their feet. When Kevin looked down, he froze once again! He hadn't realised they were actually on the edge of a cliff! It was too late to go back now. They stood there, covered in mud with their backs to the cliff face. They could suddenly hear the two wolves above them, followed by Davenport. Kevin found it hard to breathe. He closed his eyes and clenched his fists. Monkey and Katie noticed what was wrong and stood rigid. There was nothing more they could do to help their friend. He must face his own fear for, Katie thought, if he moved or called out, it would be the end for all of them! It was hard to breathe without panting, but they each had to stay still and quiet. Luckily for them, the wind was still whistling and masked their breathing.

'What's the matter now, can't you find them?' he shouted angrily. 'You mangy dogs, you are supposed to be hunters and you can't even find a scent, pathetic.' The dogs were moving in a figure of eight trying to find the scent of their victims who were only three metres below them.

'Where have they gone? Where are you, you wasters?' He spat in disgust. 'Don't think for one moment you've escaped me. I-WILL-FIND-YOU.' He ranted like a wild thing. Katie trembled with cold, fear and fatigue. Kevin's legs started to wobble and he tried to breathe calmly, whilst keeping his eyes tight shut. Monkey was taut and wide-eyed, like a zombie. One move or sound, that's all it would have taken for them to betray themselves. Davenport walked over to the edge and looked down, but there was enough overhang to conceal their bodies. He leant over and rolled his eyes from side to side. Then the old man kicked a small rock in anger and it fell centimetres in front of Katie's face...she almost screamed! They could hear him, feel his breath almost. There was a low growl in his throat, a rasping that made Katie weak. He spat and a green blob of saliva whizzed down past them. It was disgusting. She breathed quietly and slowly and kept her eyes shut whilst resting her palms on the rock face. Moments passed... She felt as though her chest would explode. Her eyes started to fill up, but she kept firm. She felt like bursting out in a full-on crying fit, but didn't!

'Crusher! Ripper! – let's look over here!' Davenport stepped away from the edge and soon they were gone. But Katie, Kevin and Monkey stood on the edge for a very long time before they decided to move. They were too scared to go back up just in case the crafty codger was waiting, hidden somewhere. The weather had ceased its bitter battle with the land and calm was now the order of the day.

'Look, he's on the bridge,' Kevin announced in a triumphant whisper. They could all clearly see Davenport and his pets making their way back to the chamber. They were hidden from Davenport's gaze by the rocky outcrop. They could see him, but he couldn't see them – for now.

'Let's get off this cliff face before he sees us,' Katie urged, and she reached over to Kevin.

'I'll hold your hand, Kev. Don't look down – just ease your way over bit by bit,' she instructed. They all eventually climbed back up and over the wall and sat down to recover from their ordeal.

'That's as close as I ever want to get to that crazy old man,' Kevin said with relief.

'I know what you mean, Kev, I thought we were goners,' Katie said with a sigh.

'What's our next move?' Monkey asked. 'We still have to get Shelley out,' he remarked.

'We know, Monkey, we haven't forgotten her,' she said sharply. 'But it's not going to be easy.'

'No, but that can't stop us...can it?' Kevin said with a smile. 'But going back is one thing, finding her is another,' he admitted.

'What do you mean, Kev?' Katie enquired softly.

'Well, I hate saying this but we only heard her voice, it could be a trick to get us back in there. Don't forget, Katie, you've got the stone. Davenport wants the stone more than anything.'

'Yeah, but Shelley is still alive, though, isn't she?' Katie said, praying she was right.

'We have to believe that, Katie,' Monkey added.

'I agree, she is still alive and waiting for us,' Kevin gently swayed his glance from Katie to Monkey. There was a pause while they thought, then Katie's eyes lit up.

'What if I just gave the stone to Davenport?' She looked around her, waiting for approval. Monkey waded in before Kevin had a chance.

'That would be suicide. Once Davenport has that stone, he then has complete power over and under Reflections. Many will die. Many will be enslaved. That must not happen, Katie. Davenport must not get possession of that stone. The future of Reflections is at stake.' He ended his words with a deep, worried look in his black eyes.

'We must make a plan to rescue Shelley and somehow stop Davenport, too. And also keep the stone safe.' Kevin didn't look convinced, even as he said it.

Chapter 16

The bargain

'I know you can hear me.' Davenport's voice boomed across the expanse of Sub Reflections, as if powered by a megaphone.

'I know you can hear me,' he repeated, and the recurring echo blended into the previous message. By this time, all three of the perpetrators were peering over a wall that butted up against the edge of the city. They were in a good position to see, but remain unseen by the enemy.

'He's standing there by the pillars that lead into the graveyard.' Monkey spoke softly, peering into the distance with bright, glassy eyes. He so wanted to kill Davenport once and for all. 'There, look, at the end of the bridge. He's standing there, smug as you like.' He indicated with his finger. He felt anger deep inside as did the others. Katie and Kevin were stooped low either side of their friend and their eyes followed the direction he stipulated. The weather had totally subsided as calm and the feeling of emptiness remained. Besides the sound of Davenport's annoying voice, there was only the wind whipping up from the depth of the canyon. The sky was clear and, without the dust clouds to obstruct the view, everything was peaceful. If it wasn't for the fact that they were in such a grave situation, taking in this view was quite a nice experience. From this vantage point, though, the headstones to the rear of the pillars were clearly visible, too, and took away some of the beauty of the landscape. The bridge linking the city to the graveyard looked a lot longer than it had previously. And deep down at the bottom of the canyon, almost out of sight and gushing along merrily, was the river, undeterred by the controversy above.

'Give me a sign that you can hear me?' he commanded gruffly, his hatred pealing through. Katie was about to shout out when Monkey stopped her. He gently gripped her shoulder with one hand and put his finger to his lips with the other, and shook his head vigorously; she didn't understand and was naive to the old man's tactics.

'No, we keep him guessing Katie,' Monkey said with importance. Kevin readily agreed with a nod. 'He doesn't really know who came to rescue her, does he? It was way too dusty to see anything or anybody clearly, so he wouldn't truly have picked out anyone in particular. He's only assuming it's us. The less he knows, the better it is for us to outfox him. Whatever he has to say, he'll have to do it without our help.' Monkey was wise and always thinking ahead. Katie then understood the tactics of secrecy in this game and was ready to play along.

'You're trying my patience,' he bellowed harshly. 'Bloody kids,' he cursed to himself. 'All right, if that's how you want to play it,' he barked angrily. 'Go get 'em, boy.' Without warning, Davenport released Ripper, one of his Razzard wolves. To Kevin, Katie and Monkey's horror, the wild wolf came surging across the narrow bridge, its eyes burning yellow and its sharp, long, green teeth bared fully and dripping saliva. Its intent was obvious: whatever it came into contact with was going to die a horrible, dark and painful death! The wolf tore at full speed across the narrow ledge. Now it could see where it was going. Now it didn't need to hold back with fear of falling over the edge. Its blood-curdling growls reverberated around them and terrified its victims even before it came into contact with them.

'Oh, my god,' Katie squeaked. Kevin had to think fast. Ripper was already half way across the bridge, just hitting the narrowest part where Katie had nearly fallen earlier. Kevin quickly looked around and his eyes fell on what he needed.

'Help me,' he snapped. 'The stones piled over there.' They instantly understood. They grabbed a handful of smooth, pebble-like stones, each about the size of a medium apple. They then quickly made their way back to the wall. To their horror, the wolf was three-quarters across the bridge and gaining speed. Kevin dropped the rest of the stones and kept one. He weighed it up in his hand skilfully and aimed. A quiet calm surrendered itself to the teenager and a wry smile filled his face. Ripper was coming to the end of the bridge; soon he would be on them.

'Kevin, Kevin, hurry up, he's nearly here,' Katie screeched in panic. Without any more delay, Kevin aimed and tossed the stone in an instant, with just about the right amount of power and accuracy. It landed with a crack on the base, just in front of the dog and instantly bounced up. It hit Ripper square on the nose and stunned him completely . . . he stopped! The stone ricocheted off his snout and sprang away down into the depths, bouncing and cracking against the canyon wall in its descent. Ripper yelped like a scalded hound, so loud it hurt their ears. He shook his dazed head and looked helpless. He wobbled in a disorien-tated state, blood pouring from each of his two nostrils and dripping red spots on the dry surface.

'Nice shot,' Monkey said in admiration and surprise. Before the wolf had time to recover, though, Kevin had launched a second missile. This one hit him on the left shoulder and this time the dog howled in pain. Kevin gave a triumphant 'Yes!' The wolf, now downbeaten, turned tail and scrambled back the way he'd come, towards a very disgruntled master. Davenport was angry and gritted his teeth in disgust.

'Listen to me! You-you cowards.' His husky tones boomed through the air like a saw cutting into tin. Ripper shot past him and he gave the dog a thump for good measure. 'You useless hound,' he scolded once again and a thought crossed his mind. A broad grin lit up his lined features. 'I have her prisoner, you know.' He spoke quietly at first and then boomed, 'I HAVE HER PRISONER! You want her back, don't you? I want the stone, simple really,' he said, as if negotiating for a contract in a business deal. 'Give me the stone and you can have the girl. Do you hear me? I'm sure even *you* can understand how simple it is.' Davenport's voice softened a little as he patronised. 'I won't harm her or you if you give me the jewel, honestly I won't!' His sickly, deceiving tones congealed on their ears. They gave each other a disgusted look as if swallowing medicine. They still kept silent; there was a long pause that Davenport gave them to reply. He waited and waited and grew impatient. Now the timbre of his voice changed to a more damning level when they didn't answer. 'If you don't comply,' he was raging this time, 'I will let the wolves have their fun with her.' Those last words hit Katie like a sledgehammer in the stomach and she felt physically ill. She sucked in air as if she couldn't breathe. Monkey thought she was going to call out and raised his hand to stop her, but she didn't. A stream of tears flourished from her eyes and streamed to her lips. Monkey automatically put his arm around her as he had done many times before to comfort her.

'I'm sorry,' he whispered in her ear. 'We can't give in to this fiend. He'll stop at nothing when he has it. You know that.' He looked at her with warmth and she rested her forehead on his shoulder.

'Do you hear me? You have one hour; I will come back here then and call you. If you don't answer, I'll bring her out and let the wolves have her in front of you. One hour,' he repeated. They saw him turn and walk back towards the chamber, and his wolves stood up and followed obediently, one limping.

'This proves it. He *does* have her prisoner,' Kevin piped up and felt hope for the first time. He looked at the others. 'This is the first proof we've had that she is still alive, and if *he* can get to her, so can we.' He beamed. 'But now that's the least of our problems,' he conceded. They all turned and sat on the ground with their backs supported by the wall. They sat quietly for quite a while, racking their brains as to what to do. The weight of guilt in carrying the stone and her friend in so much danger made Katie feel totally useless.

'Look, I have the stone, why don't we just give it to him and he'll free her. Maybe we can then snatch it back.' Katie said weakly. 'Or maybe he will keep his word and let us go.' She knew before she'd even finished the sentence that he wouldn't.

'We've talked about this, Katie. If he has the stone, what's to stop him killing us straight away? Once it's in his grasp . . . we won't get it back, I can assure you of that.' Kevin answered. 'I know this man. I know what he's capable of.' Kevin continued, with thoughts of the past. 'He kept me and Shelley locked in a room until Shadrack Scarrat came for us – before Shadrack turned good,' he added. 'He's a master at controlling other people's minds. He fooled us completely and I normally know when someone is lying to me. Davenport is quite mad, you've just seen the way he treated his own pets. What chance do you think we'd have?'

'Once he has the stone, he'll have the power to kill us anyway, and what will happen to the people of Reflections?' Monkey cut in, staring into nothingness. 'No Katie, he must not have the stone – even if we can't save Shelley . . . then we must lose the stone for ever!'

'All right then, what do we do?' Katie carried on. 'It seems impossible to even get close enough to do anything, especially with those blasted wolves', she cursed.

'I don't know how we're going to do it. We're running out of time,' Kevin said anxiously.

'All right then, let's just let him kill Shelley!' Katie answered flippantly.

'This attitude is not helping, Katie,' Monkey responded with a stare that could chill hell. Katie felt scolded.

'I'm sorry, it was a stupid, immature thing to say,' she said sheepishly. 'I'm sorry Shelley,' she said, looking at the sky.

'No, we have to come up with something that will give us time to escape with Shelley and give Davenport what he thinks is the diamond,' Monkey concluded with relish and a gleam in his dark eyes.

'A decoy, how?' Kevin simply replied with doubt written all over his face.

'I don't know, but something to occupy his mind might give us time to rescue Shelley.' Monkey shook his head and sighed. That gave Katie an idea and a smile curled her muddied lips.

'What, Katie? If you have an idea let us in on it – we haven't much time, you know,' Kevin urged.

'Where's that pool of mud, the one we rolled in?' she asked. Kevin looked bewildered.

'It's back up there somewhere. Why?' He looked blank and pointed back up the hill. 'What, you want to dive in again?' he grinned.

'Show me quickly,' she commanded 'Come on.' Kevin looked at Monkey and they both shook their heads, but made their way back anyway.

'It's a long shot, boys,' she said, with a roll of her shoulders.

'A long shot is better than no shot at all. I've learned that when you have an idea, Katie, to roll with it,' Kevin said. 'Look, that's where we climbed over the wall and hid on the ledge,' he said knowingly. 'And here's the puddle where we got covered in this filthy, stinking mud.' He retched and pointed intently. They were still covered in the drying, caked-on mess. The puddle was not so much water as a mud-pasted pie by now. 'Katie, what are we doing here?' Kevin asked. 'I hope we're not going back in there.' He cringed.

'That's exactly what we're doing,' she answered.

'Yes, Katie, but what are we looking for?' Monkey probed cluelessly.

'Look, when I was pushed in there,' and she looked directly at Kevin when she uttered the words, 'I saw something glint, I mean it's a really long shot, but there may be something in there we can use as a decoy,' she said. 'You know, for a copy of the jewel to fool Davenport. I mean he doesn't really know what size and shape it really is, does he?' she questioned, peering at the two of them. Kevin and Monkey looked at one another and nodded; they didn't have any other plan. They were still damp from the first outing, but tentatively scrambled back in the mud all the same. They pushed their hands into the squishy brown and yellow mass and pulled out handfuls of disgusting, smelly clay. Now and then, Kevin would find a small rock or Katie would find a rotten piece of wood. There were even squishy little creatures in there that made Katie jump, but she continued.

'Hey, stop, you two.' Monkey had something in his hand and he was swilling it in a smaller puddle he'd found at the base of the wall. It was cleaner than the big mud puddle and Monkey lifted out what he'd found and gave a broad smile. 'Katie, where's the jewel?' he asked, holding onto the object he'd just found. She dipped her dirty hand into her pocket and brought out the real stone, which glowed faintly. She and Monkey held them side by side. Although hers was bigger and rounder, there wasn't much difference to the untrained eye. Katie could tell straight off because she'd held it and looked at it for a long time, but to someone who hadn't seen it . . . they wouldn't know the difference!

'Oh yes-yes-yes-yes!' she screamed in delight. They moved back down the hill to the place where they were before.

'We have something to bargain with, now all we need is a good plan,' Kevin said excitedly. 'I think I've thought of something. Look, Monkey, you may have been spotted, being the last one on the bridge, but no one will have seen me. It was way too dusty, so Davenport may not even know how many of us there are.'

'Kev, what are you talking about?' Katie asked.

'You two can cross the bridge and do the swap with the stone and Shelley. Davenport won't be expecting me. I can follow and hide somewhere,' he said, his eyes filled with a strangeness that Katie or Monkey hadn't noticed before. 'I could, maybe, sneak up behind him and well . . .' He didn't say any more.

'And-and what, Kevin?' Katie was getting worried and looked at Monkey. 'Monkey, what's he talking about?' she badgered.

'I have a knife, Katie. I would have to . . . kill him!' Kevin said the words simply and without emotion.

'Kill him?' Katie hadn't really thought about that part. 'But what, really kill him . . . Murder?' She'd seen it being faked in movies on Sky. She'd seen it in a more real sense on the news, but she hadn't really seen it up front. 'You wouldn't even be allowed to carry a knife in my world, Kev. This is exactly why y-you can't do it,' she stammered. 'Monkey, tell him he can't do this.' Monkey looked at a loss.

'Katie, he has to. I've also thought about it. The man is mad and he has already killed. If we don't, then he will kill us,' he said, with a deep sense of dread. 'Remember on the bridge, Katie? He shot at us. I'll admit it was a warning shot because he couldn't take a true shot and chance killing his wolves. If it were a clear day, Katie, he would have shot and killed all three of us there and then. My world is totally different to yours, my world is survival,' Kevin answered adamantly, his eyes glazed and his teeth clenched.

'Katie, it may be the only way.' Katie was astonished at Monkey's words, her best friend. She never thought he would go against her in this way. 'Even then we may all be killed by the wolves. There isn't a good way out of this, you must accept that.' Monkey looked at her solemnly. 'I know you don't want to hear these words from me, Katie, and I'm normally the one who wants peace, but I can't see another option.'

'So we're agreed.' Kevin peered at them and Katie looked away, but she finally turned back towards him.

'I guess,' she answered reluctantly, fear in her face. Monkey felt a pang of guilt and couldn't look at her for a moment. He knew he was right and finally did look her straight in the eye as tears filled hers. She dropped her gaze and he sighed heavily and gently gripped her shoulder. Were they going to get out this time? The fearful thought swirled in her head like an angry wind. Was this actually going to be her last adventure in Reflections? Would she ever see Shelley again . . . alive? Her mind was in a state of turmoil.

'We have a plan, so let's do it,' Kevin said with confidence.

Chapter 17

Ghostly encounter

'I'm not going anywhere until I get cleaned up,' Katie announced to the utter annoyance and shock of Kevin.

'What! Are you nuts? We haven't time for this nonsense,' Kevin barked angrily. 'This is no time for girlie washing. We have a job to do.' Monkey just smiled and nodded his head, knowing full well the outcome of this situation.

'What are you grinning at?' Kevin shot Monkey a deadly stare, his face like thunder. 'Am I the only sane one here?' he raged.

'No matter what you say, Katie won't go anywhere unless she looks presentable,' Monkey said, still smiling. 'I've tried in the past to push her along, but she won't.'

'Damn right,' Katie returned with a nod and a grin that filled her face; determination shone through.

'Well, where are you supposed to get cleaned up then?' Kevin asked flippantly, folding his arms in defiance.

'I don't know, but we're all caked in mud and I don't like it.' Her obstinate nature with the obvious need to preen was not going to be ignored. If he could do this without these two, he would have, but knew he couldn't.

'This is totally ridiculous,' Kevin protested, but looked at Katie and could see that his ranting wasn't going to make a tiny bit of difference. 'All right, all right, I'll find water somewhere,' he yielded reluctantly.

'We'll all go.' Monkey joined in. 'We're not splitting up. Not now.' They got up and made their way to a part of the city that they hadn't explored. It was deathly quiet as they walked through streets of deserted houses and grand buildings. Eventually, they approached a square in which there was a cenotaph centred on a base encircled by steps. To Katie's amazement and joy, there was a figurehead and, from its mouth, free-flowing water.

'Yes!' She punched the air in approval. 'These people must have needed water as much as we do. Remember the water fountain in the cemetery?' she said. The water looked clear and was cold to the touch.

'It must be flowing from a mountain stream somewhere, to be continuously at hand to drink,' Kevin assumed, 'Obviously clever people.' Katie dipped her hands right in and swiftly the basin of water clouded in murky mud. There was a channel at the side where the water flowed on and continued through the city. As soon as her hands were clean, she held them cupped and let the water pool inside her joined palms. She lapped and drank hard and her parched throat welcomed the icy-cold liquid. She turned and quickly got a 'brain freeze' from the intense cold. Kevin laughed and did the same thing that she had just done. Monkey, laughing at the both of them, didn't seem too concerned about the temperature. When they had their fill, Katie tried as best as she could to wash off the excess mud. Kevin reluctantly did the same, and Monkey, until all three were way, way, cleaner. Their clothes were still filthy, but at least they could recognise each other now. In the midst of tidying her hair, Katie stopped what she was doing. Kevin noticed straight away that she was staring at something and he quickly followed her eyes.

'Monkey,' he whispered.

'I know, Kevin, he's been there for the last few minutes,' Monkey replied coolly. 'Keep calm and continue what you're doing.'

'Monkey,' Katie called quietly, not realising that they were staring at the same thing. 'There's someone here besides us,' she said.

'We know, Katie, stay still and don't panic,' Kevin added. Katie hated being told to 'not panic', but on this occasion she did as she was told.

To one side of the square and quietly leaning against a wall was a figure – a man of medium height, dressed in what appeared to be shabby work clothes. His brownish hair was unkempt and floppy and he looked unshaven. The really odd thing about him, though, was the fact that his whole body was partially transparent, like he was made of ice.

'B-but I can s-ee thro-ugh him,' Katie staggered through her words. 'But that's impossible. I shouldn't be able to see through him unless . . .'

'I'm confused, too, but I'm finding out anything is possible here,' Kevin said, his eyes not moving from the area where the apparition was standing.

'H-he's a gho-st,' Katie continued.

'Fascinating,' Monkey chipped in, with a degree of intrigue. 'Really interesting.'

'Scary, more like,' Katie responded hesitantly, thinking Monkey sounded like Spock from the Star Trek movies. 'What do you think he wants?' she asked, her face getting paler by the second.

'I don't know, ask him?' Kevin joked. This was something interesting that he hadn't come across before, and he was a little excited.

'You're not afraid, Kev?' Katie responded in surprise.

'Well, he's not harming us, is he? And if he is a ghost – well, he can't actually grab anything, can he? If he could or wanted to hurt us, he probably would have done so by now.' Kevin continued with a certain amount of confidence.

'I wonder what he wants with us,' Monkey pondered.

'Where did he come from is what I want to know,' Kevin added. All the time they were talking, the figure just stared in its ghostly way and then finally uttered:

'I won't harm you. I want to help you.' The apparition talked, his voice seemed amplified! Katie's heart raced as she breathed hard almost to the point of panting. Her hands began to shake and she stepped back behind her friends for protection.

'He...spoke,' she squeaked.

'Why are you here? What do you want?' Monkey took the initiative and bravely moved forward a step.

'I'm here because of the Cric,' he answered simply; his voice was as melodic as a sweeping wind. Monkey looked at Kevin and Kevin shook his head, trying to work out what he meant. Katie mouthed the word Cric and looked blankly back at the others.

'Cric, what are you talking about. What's a Cric?' Kevin asked bluntly. The ghostly form eased off the wall and stood upright.

'It's the jewel that the girl carries.' He still spoke softly, but away from the wall his body was a little harder to see. He pointed toward Katie who looked physically ill at that point. She was the one he wanted and her heart began racing. Strangely, as he spoke, it was possible to see straight through to the back of him. Katie immediately felt in her pocket for the jewel and was relieved when she grasped it in her fist.

'How on earth does he know we've got the stone? He must be in with Davenport,' Kevin whispered to Monkey. Monkey's face grew stern and he clenched his fists.

'What do you want with it?' Kevin said. 'We need it, it's ours. You're not having it to give to that mad fool, over there,' he boomed.

'I . . .' he paused for a moment and his body seemed to be floating about a couple of centimetres off the ground, 'don't want anything with it. I'm not with that mad fool either, but the Cric must not be put back.' His eyes widened and made the features of his face appear more prominent.

'What do you mean *not put back*?' Katie intervened. 'You don't want Davenport to have it either then? Where does it come from, the pattern of the chair? Is that where it came from?'

'Yes, exactly,' the ghost reasoned; its face seemed to brighten. 'It simply can't resume its place.' This made Katie feel easier and more relaxed.

'I knew it,' she uttered with more confidence. 'It

looked exactly the right fit.'

'How do you know all this?' Monkey cross-examined the ghost. The figure moved closer and everyone automatically took a step back.

'Don't come any nearer,' Kevin said abruptly, and the ghostly form stopped in mid-flow.

'Kevin, he doesn't mean to harm us or he would have by now.' Monkey reassured him and Katie. Katie, filled with more confidence, stepped from behind Kevin until all three were standing abreast.

'Come closer,' Katie said surprisingly, and waved her hand in an invite. She looked at both her friends and said, 'As you've said, if he wanted to harm us he could have by now . . . couldn't he?' she expressed towards Kevin. 'What is your name and where are you from?' she asked, as he hovered only a metre or so from her.

'Via,' he answered quite simply. 'Via of the Sand Clan.'

'Where are you from, Via – here in the city?' Katie was in full flow now and Kevin and Monkey stood silent. 'Is this place your home?'

'Yes, Sand City is my home. It's where my family and friends lived when things were . . .' He paused in thought, his face saddened. 'When there were better times. When times were simple and good,' he said, and a smile resumed on his ghostly face.

'So this place is actually called 'Sand City,' Kevin almost reluctantly slipped in and curled a smile; the three of them had only made up the name. 'Who are your people?'

'We are – were – the first settlers in Reflections. A new world to live in.' Via continued.

'There are more of you then, are there?' Kevin said, thinking they needed all the help they could get.

'Yes, we first came to Reflections and lived above ground. Things were a lot better then, life was good. We all thought we could live up there for ever without any problems.' He held back a smile. 'But then things changed. When we felt the presence of people coming to the world of Reflections, we went below ground. We wanted peace and to keep ourselves to ourselves. We are – were – a private people.' The last words seemed to hurt him.

'You are not originally of this world then?' Monkey asked.

'No, we lived on another world until 'they' came and we had to move on,' Via conceded. 'We didn't want to, but we had to.'

'They?' Katie quizzed. 'Who are they?' She was deeply enthralled.

'Plogs,' Via replied. All three were staring at Via, but upon the mention of the word Plog, this shot fear into their hearts. 'The Plogs came and invaded our world. We are a peaceful people and didn't want to be en-slaved, so we escaped and found this world. It was bar-ren and quiet and so we built another life for ourselves hoping that they wouldn't follow. They wanted what we had, the Cric.'

'So the Cric *is* yours?' Kevin said.

'Yes, it was, and they wanted it. They needed the Cric to be all powerful. But when we felt them coming, we went underground. We made this world for ourselves down here and hoped they wouldn't find us. But that didn't last as long as we'd thought. They did, eventually, discover us, enslaved us and took over our new world completely. Gryphon, their leader, became overlord and governed us. He also made us build him that chamber,' Via continued. 'He took the Cric and embedded it in his throne, but one day someone stole it. Someone from your world above.'

'Lord Fairbourne,' Monkey sighed.

'Shelley's grandfather,' Katie gushed.

'Well, Gryphon was enraged and sent most of his Plog army to get the stone back. But after a long time, they did not return. Without the Cric, his powers soon began to wane. He thought he could control us on his own with his power of persuasion. We were a simple people that did not fight. But we knew we had to defeat him or we would have been his slaves for ever. So we overpowered him and imprisoned him within the throne. Our life blood soon diminished with the loss of the Cric, too, so we eventually died. As we lost more and more, we buried everyone in the graveyard in front of the chamber,' he said sombrely.

'Those graves are all your people?' Katie felt sadness for them. 'But there are hundreds of graves over there. You mean there's no one left at all?'

'No, thousands of my people!' he added with sadness. 'So, you see, if the Cric is replaced, then Gryphon will rise again and begin another reign of terror.' Via looked fearful, even for a ghost.

'But you are already dead,' Katie said, trying to show sympathy. 'He can't harm you now, or your people.'

'It doesn't matter, his power with the Cric will be so dangerous that he will be able to control the dead and the living; no one is safe,' Via's face contorted in a grimace.

'Can your people help us?' Kevin said with hope.

'No, I am the only one that refused to let go of my persona. The rest just gave up and I buried the last of them, but with no one to bury me, I stayed like this. I don't know how, but until the Cric is returned to my world, I will stay in between worlds.' Via looked dejected. Even in his ghostly death, he was haunted by the old ruler. Katie felt a real sorrow for him.

'Then the stone must return to your world . . . end of story,' Monkey said with determination.

'But how, Monkey?' Katie asked honestly and there seemed to be no answer.

'If the stone does return by some miracle to your world, Via, how can we save Shelley? She is prisoner over there!' Kevin responded. 'Via, you can help us now.' He looked at the ghostly figure. 'Will you help us?' he asked.

'I have seen the wolves and their master. He is as vicious as they are. Of course I will help in any way I can. I don't really know what I can do, though. I can't physically fight, but I can let you know what the enemy is doing,' Via said.

'To get Shelley back and keep the stone away from Davenport is not going to be easy,' Monkey added with scepticism, 'but we have an extra pair of eyes now.' He looked at Via and nodded. Via nodded back.

'Have you seen Shelley?' Katie asked, with hope in

her eyes.

'I do not venture into the chamber, so I don't know what is in there now. But I will go in to help you.' He smiled a pale smile and popped in a startling question. 'Are you hungry? Is that a yes or a no?'

Katie's eyes almost fell out. Monkey and Kevin looked at Via with wonder, too.

'Yes, really, really, really hungry,' Katie repeated. 'Why, Via, is there *food* here?' She was excited and the word food came out with such relish.

'I know of food in Sand City. You will need strength to fight this battle,' Via explained.

'But if you and your people have been dead for years, then won't the food be rotten?' Kevin asked doubtfully. Via laughed heartily. It looked really strange watching someone transparent having a chuckle. He let out a huge belly laugh that reverberated around the square.

'It's a fruit that we used to harvest,' he said finally. 'A fruit that still grows and is fresh.' He giggled, and his eyes flashed with the enjoyment of the moment.

'We haven't much time, Via. Where do we find this fruit?' Monkey asked. 'Is it far?'

'The fruit is called a Cracto Plum. Cracto Plums are found on the outer edges of the cliffs of Sand City.' A sudden fear filled Kevin's stomach that took over from hunger.

'Don't worry, Kevin, I'll get it,' Monkey said, sensing his fear.

'The more I think of food now, the more hungry I get.' Katie's belly gave a groan of discomfort.

'Come now, it's just over here.' The ghost glided from the square and made his way along a pathway. They instinctively followed and ended up at a wall on the edge of the city. He'd been right; it was only minutes away. Via looked as though he was standing on the wall – a wall that overlooked the vast canyon, and river that occupied it.

'Here we are,' he said and showed them with a wave gesture. Monkey sprang up to the top of the wall and could see that Via was actually hovering over empty space. He immediately dug in not to slip over the edge.

'Take it easy little one,' the ghost said. Kevin and Katie stayed back and looked on. Monkey craned his neck and could see the bunches of fruit hanging precariously over the canyon. The Cracto Plum was purple in colour and was the size of a large pear or smallish melon. He began climbing out and found he hadn't lost any of his mountaineering skills. It indeed took him no time at all to shimmy over to a batch and fetch back a couple under his arm. He went back and got more until they had about three each.

'You can bite into it without peeling,' Via assured them. All three, dubious at first, sniffed, then Katie licked; there was not much taste on the outside. Kevin bit first, and when a large smile appeared, Katie and Monkey tucked in. There were no pips or stones, just mouth-watering enjoyment. For the next ten minutes there was no sound from any of them, except munching, slurping, sucking and generally devouring the fruit. Then laughter as Via looked on in curiosity.

'Wow, thiths tastht's amazthing.' Katie's mouth was so full she could barely speak. They ate every last piece and once they'd had their fill, they were ready.

'Now, down to business,' Kevin said, filled with a deep determination. Katie felt reluctance in her full stomach and knew there was no going back. Monkey wondered whether any of them would survive!

Chapter 18

Deadline

'I'm h-e-r-e.' Davenport called out from beyond the bridge. 'Time is up children. You know what you must do.' His mocking tones echoed into a dozen voices that grated across the expanse. He sounded like the child collector from the movie Chitty-Chitty Bang-Bang. His condescending tone bore down on Katie like a heavy weight. She could just about see his minute form standing in between the two huge pillars, but she was still hidden. The bridge looked foreboding, like a narrow walk of death! She cringed at the thought of what she must do to help her friend.

'Come across the bridge and hand me the stone,' he boomed from beyond. 'Then you are free to go. Your friend will also be freed,' he added simply and concisely as if giving a gift away to a pauper. Katie reluctantly handed Kevin the 'real' Cric and kept hold of the fake one. It felt empty and worthless in her grasp, like a wilted flower. The real stone had given her strength when she needed it, and physically opened doors for her to walk through. It even defended her against enemies and without it there was nothing, no defence and no hope.

'May I see it one more time?' Via asked in anticipation, a look of desperation on his face. Katie and Monkey reluctantly nodded in agreement. Kevin gently held out his upturned hand and slowly opened his palm. Via's eyes seemed to light and a real smile filled his pale face.

'Beautiful, simply beautiful!' he gushed and held his clenched hands to his face as if in prayer. 'Why must something so shiny and perfect be used for evil?' The thought made him clench his eyes shut.

'It's time,' Monkey reminded them solemnly. With those words, Katie's stomach knotted up like a snagged piece of string.

She found it hard to breathe for a moment and her hands began to tremble.

'Are you going to be OK?' Monkey asked in concern. She closed her eyes and then focused. She didn't answer, only nodded vigorously.

'I'm getting impatient, children,' Davenport responded with gritted teeth. 'Come now, time is short.' He emphasized the latter.

'If he calls us children one more time, I'll-I'll make him eat the damned stone,' Katie snarled.

'I'll wait here,' Via said and sat on a flat rock as he'd always done. Katie and Monkey made their way down the twisting pathway to the gates. They stepped through and finally showed themselves to the enemy. They both felt vulnerable and exposed, as if on stage in front of thousands of people.

'I can't do this, Monkey,' she said, but a squeeze of her hand made her stronger.

'Come on, we can do this. We *have* to do this,' he said, a tremble in his voice. 'There is no other way. No other way.' He repeated this as if to convince himself.

'At last-at last, now come on, come on over,' he was abrupt, but gave the impression he was inviting them over to a party. There was joy in his tones.

'Wow, Monkey, he's weird,' Katie said. They walked to the edge of the cliff and stood at the foot of the bridge. Katie took a deep breath before she went any further.

'I'll go first, Monkey,' Katie said, plucking up courage. 'I'm not scared.' She said this with as much venom as she could muster, even though her knees were almost knocking together. 'I'm not scared of him. I'm not scared of anyone.' As she said it, a cliffkreeper flew up from the canyon and squawked loudly as it passed them. Katie let out a scream that could be heard in the next country. Monkey, without her knowing, was shocked at first and then stifled a laugh.

'Wait!' Davenport demanded, his voice boomed. 'Where is the other one? 'Where is the boy?' He stood, waiting for an answer.

'There *is* no other one! It's only me and Monkey,' Katie recoiled tentatively.

'I'm sure there were three of you,' he said, scratching his head, not totally convinced. 'All right, maybe not.' He sounded a little confused. 'Come on over and don't try anything stupid. My dogs are only waiting for my command and you know what they are capable of,' Davenport said with a sickly smile. Katie and Monkey then realised that laying on the base of each of the pillars were his two Razzard Wolves. Crusher and Ripper looked as ferocious as they had ever done. Even from this long distance they looked a frightening and deadly sight.

They walked timidly across the narrow stone path toward Davenport. Katie looked down, and the sheer drop to the canyon below felt even more threatening than any other time they'd crossed.

'Oh boy, what are we doing here, Monkey?' Katie gasped.

'You know why we're here Katie. This is the very reason I brought you back – because you could be strong for Shelley.' This gave her extra resolve and a strained smile replaced the stiff, worried look she was carrying. As they eventually crossed the middle section and most narrowed part, Davenport shouted and made Katie flinch. She almost stumbled over until Monkey grabbed her blouse. She put the palm of her hand to her chest and breathed hard.

'Don't worry, Katie, I've got you,' he assured her, breathing a little heavier.

'I wish he'd just shut up,' she snapped. 'This is hard enough to do as it is. We always seem to stumble at this point. Monkey, I vow, once we've successfully completed our mission, I'm never stepping on this bridge again.' This made Monkey crack a smile and that definitely made Katie feel easier. They shuffled along the remaining section of the bridge and were almost at the end.

'Move it – we haven't got all day,' Davenport barked impatiently.

'Do you want this stone or not, you bloody idiot?' Katie cursed angrily, to the complete surprise of Davenport.

'Wha . . . what the . . .' Davenport was disorientated for a second or so.

'Shout like that again and I may fall over the edge and so will the stone – this precious, precious stone –

so keep quiet until we get to the end,' she added, with a slice of grit in her voice.

'Well I . . . oh, all right, just keep moving,' he babbled, wondering whether he had been scolded or not.

'Katie, you go girl. I didn't know you had it in you. Well, you told him,' Monkey said sharply. By now, they were almost at the end and Katie stopped! Davenport looked on in displeasure.

'What are you doing, girl, we haven't time for this crap? Keep moving. I said keep moving, girl,' he shouted. Katie could see Davenport's twisted and angry face. The wolves, too, had moved to his side now, giving the aggressor a united front. Their eyes burned yellow and cut through her like a knife. And as they bared their sharp, stained teeth, Katie flinched and shuddered, but kept her cool.

'Where is Shelley?' she said simply, but directly, and stared unflinchingly into Davenport's eyes. He was stunned; no one had spoken to him in this manner for years, except when Shadrack Scarrat was alive.

'She's here – stop stalling. Now come on and give me the stone,' Davenport insisted with a grunt. Monkey said nothing, but followed her lead.

'I don't see her! Do you see her, Monkey?' Monkey shook his head without saying a word. 'I can only see your ugly face, and those dogs. Where is Shelley?' Katie demanded, this time a real fire in her voice. Her eyes were still focused on Davenport, who felt vulnerable for the first time. He reasserted himself.

'Get over here and give me that damn stone,' he insisted, 'or I'll come over there and take it from you.' He seemed genuine. Katie noticed he was carrying a rifle hitched on his shoulder, which he removed and pointed at her.

'Katie, what are you doing? He'll kill you. You know he'll kill you.' Monkey whispered in panic. 'He's not messing about,' he said with a tremble. 'What are you doing, girl? Don't call his bluff.' He repeated, almost choking at the same time.

'Monkey, I know what I'm doing.' But Monkey could hear the fear in her voice, and her body was a mass of jelly.

'OK, I've always trusted you,' he whispered meekly. 'If you say you know what you're doing, then you know what you're doing. Good grief.'

'Put that gun away...now!' she barked. 'Or would you like me to drop this over the edge.' She slipped her hand into her pocket and pulled out the shiny jewel. She then coolly extended her arm over the edge, with the stone in her fist. She stood there with the mock intention of dropping it! A wry smile loomed on her face at the power she held in her grip. Davenport unconsciously reached out for it and then realised and pulled back. His face was taut and pensive. Unsure what to do, he stumbled over his words.

'Uh, er . . . all right, all right, I'll get her. Don't do anything stupid, girl, I'm warning you.' He was nervous and Katie felt in control for the first time. The old man scampered off at a fair rate and left the dogs guarding the pair of them. To Monkey and Katie's surprise, Davenport walked over to one of the pillars and slipped behind it. The next thing he emerged with was a figure bound at the hands. Katie breathed in and out rapidly, as did Monkey . . . it was, in fact, Shelley! She was actually alive!

He led her to where the dogs were; Katie's heart flipped. She could barely breathe, excitement filled her whole being.

'Shelley, Shelley, are you all right? Has he hurt you?' She was in pieces. Great, bulbous tears streamed down her face. Monkey was also filled with emotion.

'Yes-yes, I'm fine,' she answered, but sounded tired and weak.

'What have you done to her, you evil man?' Monkey shouted angrily. 'You'll pay for this, you-you monster.' He ranted uncontrollably.

'She's fine, as you can see, now hand me the stone,' Davenport responded flippantly.

'I won't ask again or I will push her over.' He walked to the edge and held her over by her arm. Shelley screamed and began sobbing as tears streaked down her dirty face. Her eyes widened and terror filled her tiny face. It was a different ball game now. Davenport was in control once again.

'No . . . no, don't please.' Katie disintegrated like a sand castle in the wind; she couldn't bluff any more; it was a lot more real now. 'I'm coming, please don't hurt her.' She put the stone back into her pocket and continued across the bridge with Monkey shuffling behind. Davenport pulled Shelley back in and she fell to her knees. He gave a hearty laugh.

'Thought you could outsmart me, did you girl?' he rasped. Once Katie got to the end of the bridge, Davenport was waiting eagerly with an outstretched hand. Katie now truly understood what she really had in her pocket and felt weak. This is a lame plan, she suddenly realised, and now it would only be a matter of time before she's found out. Her mind was in turmoil. Reluctantly, she pulled out the stone for the last time and placed it in his huge spade of a hand. He grasped it tightly and grinned. She then forgot everything and stooped to the floor and hugged Shelley with all her might. They were both in floods of tears when they embraced.

'Are you truly all right Shelley? What has he done to you?' Katie asked with glistening eyes. Shelley lifted her head; there were dark patches under her eyes and no spark of the old Shelley in her expression. She looked ill and burned out.

'Oh, Shelley, I'll get you out of this if it's the last thing I do,' Katie promised.

'You're going nowhere, girl,' Davenport laughed out loud. 'Did you think I was going to just let you, that stupid monkey, and that little princess go? You must be stupider that I thought. I am going to rule this world and the one above. I will be king of both Reflections. I deserve it for all my efforts over the years. *You* will be my maidservants and I'll find a use for *him*.' He pointed towards Monkey. 'Or not, I'll have to see.' He gave a big belly laugh as he said it. 'Maybe a meal for my pets, eh boys?' He sneered, and Monkey swallowed hard.

'But you said you would let us go,' Katie reasoned. 'You promised you would let us go once you had the stone. You liar...LIAR!' She screamed and sprang for him only to be beaten back by his pack of dogs.

'Don't believe everything I say, girl . . . except for the

maidservant part.' He laughed out loud again. 'Now get up and come with me; we have a presentation to perform,' he said with relish.

'What presentation, you twisted, sick, pathetic excuse for a human?' Katie screeched in full flow. 'What are you talking about?' She was ranting.

'Why, my crowning glory on the throne, of course. The placing of the stone and the power that comes with it. I am King Davenport, don't you understand? Don't you know what this means. Everyone will bow to me. I've waited and killed and now it's all mine.' He said this with real conviction.

'You can't,' Katie pleaded. 'The stone must not be put back.'

'Not be put back? Just watch me girl,' he said. 'Now move, the three of you.' This time he was pointing the rifle again and the added threat of the wolves gave his order even more substance. What were they to do? Katie thought. Kevin had a knife, but Davenport had his rifle and the two nastiest creatures ever created at his disposal. Once Davenport found out about the fake Cric, then he would take the real one from Kevin and kill him.

'We're not going anywhere until you've untied Shelley,' Katie almost spat at him.

'What, you're in no position to demand anything, girl. Don't you see I've got the gun and the mad dogs. Where do you get off in telling me what to do?' He looked confused, as if trying to convince himself. I still have a little power over him, she thought.

'Look, you want to be King, Lord or whatever right, yeah?' Katie was on a roll.

'Uh . . . yeah!' Davenport answered with a note of uncertainty.

'Well then, taking off this stupid rope won't make any difference, will it?' Katie was filled with a new courage; she had to because her friend was in such a weak state. Davenport was trying to take hold of the situation without much success.

'Now look here, girlie,' he responded weakly. Monkey and Shelley looked on in sheer amazement. He was buckling, so Katie capitalised.

'Be honest, we're not exactly going to run away with a rifle pointed at us and two wolves breathing down our necks, are we?' She stood tall and had Davenport at a great disadvantage.

'OK, OK,' he said, puffing out his chest, trying to show some authority. 'Untie her and let's get on with this. I've had enough delay,' he bellowed and Katie could see this was only as far as she could go. She couldn't stall any longer. Where was Kevin? Shelley held out her dirty hands and smiled at her friend. Katie tugged and pulled at the knots until they yielded and the rope fell away. Her wrists were snagged and burned by the abrasive quality of the rope. Shelley rubbed her wrists and winced at the pain. She flexed her wrists with the freedom of being rope-free. She gave Katie a broad smile and Katie saw her old friend return.

'No more stalling, now move.' Davenport soon had things back on track and now all they could do was obey and wait!

Chapter 19

Attack

Katie, Shelley and Monkey were being walked down the middle of the graveyard, but not of their own choice. Davenport was trailing behind, his rifle held aloft like a hunter. There was no chance of escape as his faithful wolves were flanking each side of the party, too. Their guttural growling made Katie shake as the two canine menaces flicked their gaze in the direction of the prisoners. The sky was overcast and a slight wind danced in the loose sand around their feet. There was a smell of dampness in the air, that warm, damp air that came after a great storm. How on earth were they going to get out of this, Monkey was now pondering. There's nowhere to go. They couldn't outrun the dogs and of course they would never be able to disarm Davenport. How in heaven's name would Kevin be able to overcome the old man? This was going to be a foolhardy attempt and the outcome was inevitable.

'Where's Kevin?' Shelley whispered to Katie. 'Is he all right?' Katie kept her arm warmly around Shelley's shoulder, for friendship and actual support.

'You're better off not knowing, Shell,' Katie replied bluntly and gave her a worried look.

'Why, is he somewhere out there, Katie? Come on Katie, tell me! What's happening?' Shelley was most insistent when she wanted to know something. She absent-mindedly darted her eyes around to see if she could actually spot Kevin lurking somewhere. Realising that their captor was watching, she stopped. She mouthed the words, 'Where is he?' to Katie.

'H-he's following us and waiting to attack Davenport, with a knife!' she blurted back in a whisper, 'I think, I hope, he doesn't go through with it though.'

'What!' Shelley raised her voice in anger and then realised what she'd done. She tensed and a spasm gripped her stomach.

'Are you all right, Shell?' Katie asked, concerned.

'Yeah, just a little hungry. I haven't eaten since yesterday; anyway, never mind that now,' she said. Davenport looked at both of them and said nothing. He just grumbled to himself and beckoned with his rifle for them to keep moving.

'Did all of you agree to this? I don't believe it. Kevin is not a killer,' Shelley said, as quietly as she could without getting herself noticed. 'He can't become a murderer. Kevin is not a killer,' she repeated and felt sick. 'I won't allow this to happen. I simply won't.' She hissed at Katie. 'I would never believe that you would agree with such a thing.'

'I know what you're saying, Shell, but what else are we going to do then . . . you tell me!' Katie barked back, in the quietest way she could. 'He's going to kill us all, you know.'

'What are you two up to there?' Davenport leaned closer and poked Katie in the back with the barrel of his rifle. 'I hope you're not trying to plan something, or maybe you should make a break for it,' he said with a snigger. 'Just keep moving.'

'Ow, that hurt,' she responded ominously, rubbing her back.

'There's no need to hurt anyone, Davenport. Leave them alone.' Monkey chipped in angrily.

'Shut up vermin, or you, I'll shoot without a thought. Dirty disease-carrying animal,' Davenport said and pointed his rifle at him. 'I've never trusted you since you betrayed Scarrat,' he said. Monkey kept quiet, but the hate was building.

'We're just catching up on old times, that's all,' Shelley lied unconvincingly to defuse the situation and bring the attention back to her. 'You'll regret that one day, Davenport. You really will. I'll be in charge once again, believe me,' she retaliated.

'You're in no position to threaten me, so no more chatting, just walk! I have the gun, remember,' he growled sharply. At that point, the wolves began acting up, howling and yapping. They started baring their teeth and snarled in unison. They also began looking further on up the trail and weaving about in a pensive action. The fur on their backs stood on end and they were ready to attack.

'What's the matter with you two, why are you acting so nervous? There's nothing out there, you fools,' Davenport rasped. 'You're supposed to be vicious guard dogs, not scared puppies.' He said, 'Stupid dogs – why am I surrounded by idiots?' But the two wolves weren't listening and were edging away from the party and moving further up the track. They separated and wove between the headstones, sniffing and darting their evil eyes.

'Where the hell are you going?' He was lost for a moment. 'Get back here before I really get mad. Crusher, Ripper . . . come back *now*.' He bellowed and then stopped. 'Wha...what's that?' He changed his pitch completely and his voice softened. He stood transfixed. His three prisoners were already looking into the distance. They couldn't make it out at first. There seemed to be someone standing at the entrance of the chamber, but it was too far away to see exactly who or what it was. The wolves didn't care, though, now they were at full stride, and met in the centre of the road, snarling heavily as they sped onward. Monkey, Katie and Shelley were trying to fathom out what was happening, too. They didn't click on the opportunity for a moment, then it dawned on them, there was now only Davenport to consider. There were three of them, surely they could do something. This was the perfect time to overwhelm the old man and maybe steal his weapon. But where was Kevin?

'Get back here, you crazy dogs; get back here now before I shoot you.' But it was too late – the dogs were already bounding towards the chamber like wild things. They moved quickly and weren't far from it. In the middle of all the confusion and with Davenport's attention compromised, it happened! From behind one of the gravestones he leapt out, with dagger in hand. Kevin grabbed Davenport around the neck with his left arm and pushed the point of his knife into the unsuspecting kidnapper's back. He was only fourteen, but easily as tall, if not a bit taller, than the old man. Kevin's eyes were bright and savage as he held Davenport in a tight grip. With the surprise of the attack, Davenport lost grip of his weapon and it fell to the ground with a thunk! Shelley screamed, as did Katie. Monkey, although expecting some action, was all too shocked! Kevin grappled with Davenport and pressed the point of the knife into the small of his back with more pressure. His heart was pounding in his ears. He was panting like a crazed dog and the fear of passing out was overwhelming.

'Aaargh… I knew there were more than two of you. Stupid, really stupid.' Davenport gave a guttural retch in the back of his throat. He was shocked and humiliated at being taken by surprise – especially by a kid, be it a very tall kid.

'Stay still, old man,' Kevin ordered as he applied more pressure again with the blade to the old man's spine. Every sinew, every nerve ending seemed to be set at breaking point.

'OK, take it easy, son.' Davenport said patronisingly. 'We can work something out,' he responded, his voice trembling.

'Don't 'son' me – you're no father of mine, old man,' Kevin raged. He looked possessed by some evil force. His eyes were wide and blazing, full of madness. His lips were parted, baring clenched teeth. Katie didn't recognise him at all. This was a totally new side to him. He was frighteningly realistic. Was it just an act? Or did he really have murderous intent? It was way too frightening for all of them to comprehend.

'Arrgh,' Davenport retched again. 'OK, sorry, why don't you ease back with that knife, boy?' He sneered as he said it, knowing it would enrage the youth.

'What are you trying to do, you old fool, get yourself killed in record time? I'm not messing, believe me. I will kill you.' Kevin surged, feeling a power inside like he'd never felt before. He was scared, but it was also a buzz, too. He was lost in his new role as a thug and everything else around him was immaterial. He was normally the goody-goody type, but this new power felt . . . good!

'Kevin, you can't do this. Kevin, listen to me, you can't do this,' Shelley cried as she made her way to his side. At the sight of her, he almost buckled. His heart was screaming out to her, but he couldn't let it engulf him.

'Stay back, Shel, you want to get out of this, don't you? Well, this is the only way,' Kevin blasted; he was gasping for breath. He didn't even believe what was coming out of his own mouth. His heart was filled with fire and he felt like a man for the first time in his life. His hand felt clammy as he continued to grip the handle.

'K-Kevin you're s-scaring me,' Shelley stuttered nervously. Monkey had been quiet up until then, but uttered:

'They're coming back. I can hear them. The wolves – they're coming back, Kevin.' His voice sounded damning at first and then it began lifting in alarm. 'Come on, Kevin, they're almost here. Do it . . . do it now!'

'Monkey, don't egg him on or something bad will happen. What's the matter with you? This is not the Kevin and Monkey I remember.' Katie broke into the conversation, deeply shocked by what she was hearing. Monkey gave her a stern glare.

'Get the gun, GET THE GUN, QUICKLY!' Kevin exploded. Everyone was in a state of bewilderment. Monkey reached forward and with trembling hands lifted the rifle off the ground.

'Kevin, you can't do this.' It was Via who spoke this

time; his soft tone and ghostly image appeared right next to him. Shelley was astonished at what she was seeing. There was a quiet moment, like a rift in time and for a split second Kevin was flustered and he unknowingly eased off with the knife. This gave Davenport the chance he'd been waiting for all along. He broke free from Kevin's grip and snatched the weapon away from Monkey's hand. Kevin came back to his senses and tried to grip the old man again, but it was too late. In a flash, he'd spun round and was pointing the rifle at Kevin and demanding the knife. Kevin was in two minds, but the end of Davenport's barrel was millimetres from his face and he had no choice but to relinquish his weapon. Davenport then sported a huge smile, a smile of victory.

'I've got all of you now. I can't believe it, but here you all are. You had your chance, boy, and you blew it.' He let out a huge laugh and then his demeanour turned deadly serious. 'Drop the knife or you'll drop with it; believe me, I'm not afraid to use this,' he said and his eyes confirmed what his mouth had uttered. Feeling sheepish and broken after his change of personality, he did as he was told. Davenport stooped to the ground, still pointing the weapon, and duly picked up the blade and tucked it into his belt. The wolves came charging in and Davenport scolded them severely before taking control once more.

'All right, you've had your fun – now let's get to the chamber without any more little problems. I've got everything. I've got it all.' He ranted, but Kevin reciprocated with a look of sheer disgust. They had no choice now but to do as they were told. So all of them, including Via, began floating to the chamber. All of them now wore glum faces, except for Davenport. He was already rejoicing at becoming the new King of Reflections even before he got there.

'I now bow to no one,' Davenport mumbled under his breath. 'Reflections is mine.' No one said a word all the rest of the way, except for Shelley.

'Katie, who is this?' she asked, pointing to Via, but Davenport screamed from behind and everyone fell silent. Everything they had tried to do to stop it was lost. They stood before the chamber entrance and reluctantly walked in, one by one, until everyone was inside. What fate lay ahead for them now? They slowly walked through the first passageway and into the main chamber. The throne stood waiting.

'Sit in those chairs and don't move. I may have to turn away from you to do this, but these dogs haven't eaten for a while,' Davenport said with a devilish grin. They sat on the stone seats and waited in anticipation, each of them knowing the ruby wasn't going to work. But what were they going to do then? This truly was going to be the end!

Chapter 20

A dark turn

Davenport was the happiest he'd ever been in his whole miserable existence. Everything had now fallen into place and no one could stop him ruling Reflections. He'd even begun humming a little tune as he made his way to the throne. He had a smile on his face and a skip in his step. Crusher and Ripper, his two obedient wolves, sat each side of the grand chair; they resembled the Sphinx guarding the Egyptian Pyramids. Their expressions were ferocious, eyes penetrating, darting in the direction of the prisoners. Each one was waiting and salivating to tear their victims apart. The five captives sat motionless, Kevin, with his head bowed and mind working nineteen to the dozen, Shelley looking nervously at Katie, and Katie staring back trying to smile but not quite making it. Monkey was too scared to look into the girls' eyes after the performance he'd put on earlier. He felt disgusted with himself, but he had no excuse because his animal instinct screamed survival.

Via didn't have to be there at all – he was a ghost after all and he could have floated away. But he knew once Davenport had got hold of the real stone then his own existence would be turned to slavery again. He would be under the rule of the new overlord for ever, so in his own ghostly way he was trying to think of something to help. There was no point in any of them trying to escape; they couldn't outrun the dogs and where would they escape to anyway?

Think, think, Kevin told himself. Davenport picked the stone out of his pocket and began slotting it gently into the centre of the pattern. Everyone looked on with bated breath, there was a deadly silence. Each of the prisoners' eyes were as wide as saucers as they waited with bated breath; but to Davenport's utter annoyance – it wouldn't go in!

'Hmmm,' he mumbled as he tried this way and that. However hard he pushed, it just wouldn't fit . . . it was too big! He fumbled and twisted at every angle, but it just wouldn't go.

'That's strange.' He pondered for a moment, then it hit him and his body stiffened and began to shake. His grey, hairy strands began vibrating under the intense pressure of his temper. He turned around and anger oozed from every pore.

'Where is the real stone, this one is a fake, but you know that already . . . don't you?' he bellowed through gritted teeth, and strings of saliva ejected from his mouth. Katie felt guilt-ridden and it showed from her open mouth. Shelley looked even more confused than she did before. She quickly shot Katie a glance and Katie rolled her eyes as if to say, well that plan didn't work too well. Kevin was sitting upright now and looking directly at Davenport.

'Come on, who's got it?' He was raging. 'This is getting very boring, children – you've pushed me too far. Either give it to me now or you'll all regret it.'

'Isn't that the one?' Katie tried to say with innocence, but it just came out flat and not believable.

'You know very well, girl, this isn't it. You've tricked me for the last time.' He was at his most deadly now, like a cornered animal. He stood before Katie, showing the stone in the palm of his hand.

'I have it. I have the real one.' Everyone looked at Kevin in disbelief as he blurted the words.

'No you haven't Kevin, I have it.' Katie responded. 'You know that I do.'

'No you don't, neither of you do. I have it,' Monkey piped up proudly.

'No, I have it,' Via said with a nervous chuckle. Davenport was confused and paused for a second to recollect his thoughts. He walked straight over to Shelley and pointed the rifle at her, point blank between her eyes. Everyone stopped joking around.

'Hold on, please don't hurt her,' Kevin pleaded, 'Honestly, I have it, look.' With that, he reached into his pocket and produced the gem. Everyone, including Via, was aghast. All eyes were on Kevin's hand.

'Well, that makes good sense boy; hand it to me!' Davenport smiled hungrily, he reached out and Kevin placed it in the centre of his palm. Katie shuddered and almost reached out for it herself, but it was already in the possession of its new master. In the next moment, it was as if the wind was knocked out of everyone's sails. There was no more stopping him now. He had the wolves, the weapons and now the 'Cric.' Out of all these possessions, none of them actually belonged to him. The rifle was formerly Shadrack Scarrat's and the wolves were formerly his pets. The stone was part of Via's own people's history and even the knife was Kevin's. But once he placed that stone in the hole, then everything would be his forever! Davenport was on cloud nine. His heart beat with a new excitement.

'Davenport, please don't do it. It's too much power for one person to handle,' Shelley pleaded. 'Look what it did to my father and grandfather; it nearly drove them mad. Please, you can still be King of Reflections; we'll all worship you. You don't need the stone for that power. I'm giving it to you,' Shelley declared. Davenport stopped and thought for a moment, but shrugged it off like an old overcoat.

'I don't care, the time has come,' he said with relish and walked over to the throne once more. Kevin stood up to try and stop him, but was reminded to stay where he was by the two Razzard Wolves. They stood up ready to pounce at the command of their mad master.

'Kevin, it's too late . . . it's all over,' Monkey sighed, shaking his head in disbelief.

'No, it can't be,' Shelley squeaked.

'There must be another way,' Katie sobbed. Via bit his lip, trembled slightly, and helplessly looked on. Davenport joyfully leant forward and nervously placed the Cric into its home and waited... It took some time before anything happened and then it started!

The stone began to glow, exactly the same as when Katie placed it in the door of the passageway. So she knew, with a sinking feeling in her heart, that it was all beginning to work. There was no stopping it now!

'Oh no, no,' she sobbed and went to get up in protest, but was also beaten back by the wolves. If only I had my knife, Kevin thought. Davenport immediately sat on the throne and gripped the arms as if waiting to take off on a mad roller coaster ride. His eyes were on fire and a taut grin emerged on his aged face; he looked satisfied. The glowing orange Cric evolved into a deep red and further into a pale orange and then bright yellow. With every colour change, it got brighter and brighter. It became painful to look at, so everyone in the room shielded their eyes. Even the wolves turned away from the searing light. There emitted a hum like that of a big generator bursting into life. Davenport was in a state of sheer ecstasy, he was going to become ruler of all Reflections. The excitement was overwhelming. The adrenalin coursed through his veins and a new Davenport was about to be reborn. He breathed in hard as if his last breath were about to be sucked from his body. The vibration of the stone began a reaction that was shaking the chamber. Debris fell from above and clattered on impact on the cold, stone floor. A flowing wind erupted from within the chamber, blowing Davenport's body and rippling at his clothes. He had to hold fast just to stay in the chair, the look of joy quickly fading from his terrified features. He was then unceremoniously catapulted from the throne and tossed across the room. His heavy body thudded against the wall and crumpled into a heap on the ground. Everyone else was still shading themselves from the brilliant light.

'What's happening, Kevin?' the girls screamed in unison.

'I don't know. I can't see anything,' he bellowed.

'Don't look into the light, everyone,' Monkey screeched. 'Hold fast and don't look into the light,' he repeated and as he said it, things began to calm. The room dulled from a blaze of light to a glow. This gave the captives a chance to see, once their eyes adjusted to the light. Slowly, things started to take shape and make sense. Kevin noticed Via first and called him, but he didn't respond. The spirit figure was staring ahead. So everyone did the same and their eyes fell upon a new figure. The figure was sitting on the throne, but it wasn't Davenport! Where was Davenport? The two Razzard wolves, Crusher and Ripper, instinctively leapt at the throne to attack this new threat, but to their peril. They were instantly reduced to piles of dust from a wave of deadly energy directed straight at them.

'Wow. Via, who is that?' Kevin probed, peering at this new being. He was relieved slightly at the demise of the brutes, but also curious at the figure itself.

Sitting on the throne was an apparition more than an actual body. It was a well-rounded frame made up of a bulbous torso, draped in a toga of sorts. Its head was large, looking more like a boxer dog than anything else. It had green, beady eyes where eyes would normally be found on a human. There were also layers of floppy skin, folding down from its forehead to its puffy cheeks. In the centre of its weird face were two holes; Kevin presumed these were nostrils, but no nose. A huge mouth appeared at the bottom, gaping like a wound, but not speaking. Continuing down its head and protruding from two sides were its shoulders, large, oversized. Its body seemed to fill the stone seat and beyond. His legs, which made him look partly human, were thick and hairy and ended at a pair of wide, slabbed feet. His feet were supported by thin strappy sandals and thick, sausage-like toes were bursting through. The odd thing was that its humongous body seemed the same way as Via's body . . . translucent. It wasn't a solid shape at all and this intrigued Kevin. You could easily make out the chair that it sat on, even though he covered it completely.

'It's G-Gryphon,' Via stammered, almost unable to say the word. To say he looked pale was impossible as he really was anyway. But, all the same, he was terrified.

'Oh, this is bad,' Kevin responded, realising who this person was.

'Yes, yes it is,' Via reluctantly added with sadness. 'My people are back under his rule. They don't deserve this, why can't he leave them rest in peace?' He was distraught.

'What are we going to do?' Shelley was scared and shocked.

'OBEY ME!' Gryphon interrupted with a low, guttural groan. His echoed tones hacked through the air like a serrated blade cutting through tin. 'Simply obey me.' He beamed a wide and satisfied smile. 'Oh, it feels good to be living again.'

'B-but you're supposed to be dead,' Via added again, with deep regret.

'Ah Via, well it's been a long time since you killed me.' A sneer filled his bloated face. 'I have a special place for you in my new reign as Lord. You will be my man servant for eternity.' He said this with relish.

'Every day, you will regret existing and you two strange female creatures will be my handmaidens.' He looked satisfied with himself.

'No way, creepy, I'm not serving you with anything. Are all old men power mad?' Katie said, joining in the conversation, looking as though she was going to throw up.

'Be quiet, servant, you are already beginning to annoy me. You will all speak when spoken to and not another word will leave your lips,' Gryphon commanded. 'You will also obey your new master . . . I am now fully your ruler. I am going to change everything, firstly . . .'

'Via,' Kevin whispered while letting Gryphon carry on with his continuing list of boring threats. Via turned quickly and saw Kevin was mulling something over.

'What is it?' Via mouthed back.

'Why is he see-through? Shouldn't he be a solid form?' he asked honestly.

'Because he is not yet complete, he has . . .' Via stopped what he'd started to say, there was a ghostly look of terror in his milky eyes. 'He cannot be allowed to continue his reign.' Via's voice was getting louder and Kevin could see he was about to do something. Things were going from bad to worse. In the next few minutes, Kevin knew that everything he knew as normal would change for ever.

Chapter 21

Revolt

Via, filled with fear and anger, stood up and faced his nemesis. In his entire ghostly refrain, he didn't look much of a threat to begin with. Unaware of the impending confrontation, Gryphon carried on with his new demands.

'Hold your tongue!' Via demanded with conviction and stood his ground. At that moment, all eyes were trained on the ghost in question. Gryphon was taken aback and faltered for a moment and then regained his overbearing persona.

'Stop whatever you are doing, Via, before you regret it,' Gryphon responded, with all the backlash of an army general. At that point, Kevin, Katie, Monkey and Shelley rose to their feet. Fear was in their hearts, but the fear of what might happen if they didn't stand their ground was even stronger.

'We don't want you here, Gryphon. Go now while you still can,' Via insisted.

'What do you think you are doing? Sit down before I lose my temper and kill you all as you stand!' Gryphon looked angry but agitated; he didn't expect such a challenge. Especially from a bunch of minors, a puny animal and a former enemy that he'd already dealt with and killed his race on previous occasions.

'You don't have any authority here, your rule is over,' Via exploded with venom, feeling an ever stronger determination well up inside. Gryphon, still in a ghostly form, raised his right arm in retaliation.

'I have warned you, but as usual you don't listen,' he said as he sent a series of brilliant white impulses from the tips his fingers which totally engulfed Via's whole body. This surge of power physically hurt Via, it weakened him instantly. It wrapped around his body and he crumpled to the ground like a discarded newspaper. He screamed in agony and his body, though partially transparent, began to erode and fade.

'Aaaargh,' Via screeched in sheer tortured pain, his form breaking down with the pressure of Gryphon's attack. This gave Gryphon enormous pleasure, feeling the power surge through his body once again. A smile lifted his spirits and his eyes gleamed. Via squirmed and struggled on the floor of the chamber, looking defeated.

'Huh, thought you could overpower me . . . I am Gryphon, ruler of all that I survey and beyond.' He was beginning to rant like a mad thing.

'No, stop; leave him alone.' Shelley's cries were secondary in the background. 'You're hurting him.' She fell to her knees and tried to comfort him somehow, but his form was not solid and she couldn't help him. Tears streamed down her dirty face as she whimpered. Via's face contorted in the pressure of the torture.

'You bully, what a tool!' Katie shouted with disgust. 'Stop it, stop it, you're killing him.' But her attempt to stop the attack fell on deaf ears. Gryphon continued with his torture and seemed to be relishing every moment. Kevin burst forward to stop Gryphon somehow, but he was too quick for the teenager. He raised his left arm and pointed his fingers directly at him. He, too, was subjected to a surge of energy that threw him across the floor, just as Davenport had been. Kevin luckily fell short of the wall and landed on his back. Unlike Davenport, he wasn't too badly hurt and stayed conscious but dazed. Next. it was Monkey's turn, but his small body didn't even get a chance to lunge at the new lord and he was forced to sit on the stone chair and couldn't move. Via was falling apart, literally; his body was slowly stripping away; the two girls helplessly looked on in floods of tears.

'You're killing him. Stop it, stop it,' they sobbed. Gryphon, however, was enjoying his new-found energy.

'I am Lord, I am Lord.' He was laughing hysterically, like a mad thing. 'Bow to me . . . bow to me.'

Via was almost gone, his body had diluted to a flimsy, faded photo and Gryphon seemed to be getting stronger. His body was sapping power from the stone and taking whatever life force Via had left. Kevin was back on his feet, still partially out of it. The two girls were crying hysterically and Monkey was helplessly glued to the chair! All was lost it seemed. Kevin shook his head and focused on what could he do. This was one impossible situation.

Then he noticed something! A feeling at first, strange warmth inside. Healing warmth that you would normally get from medicine. Then he saw it; a single glowing form entering the chamber. Where it had come from he didn't know. In all the confusion of screams and chanting and the excruciatingly horrible sound of Gryphon's power surges, no one had noticed it. It was the calmest thing in the cavern. He stared at it with a sense of wonder and deep curiosity. It took his attention from all the evil that was taking place. It looked of the same features as Via, but smaller, like a boy. Another strange thing began to happen in the chamber. The brilliantly bleached glow from Gryphon's fingers faded slightly to a milky colour. Gryphon was on such a high he didn't even notice that his new-found power was beginning to wane and drain away. Kevin kept his eye trained on the newcomer and then to his astonishment saw another figure emerge from behind him. This one rose up to a taller height, as if morphing from the child's body. It was obvious to Kevin now that it was an adult. They were both transparent; like Via but a softer glow, an angelic glow, a comforting inner light. With this second appearance, the energy from Gryphon's fingers paled significantly more. Via now also began to slowly regain his form.

Katie and Shelley noticed this, but not the intrusion of the other people. More of Via's people filtered into the chamber. Kevin realised that they must be the people from the many graves outside the chamber. They must have felt Via's pain and come to help, he thought. Gryphon noticed, firstly, his power draining and then the infiltration of the dead town's folk surrounding him. Many, many more poured in, like sand through a sieve.

'Stop where you are or I'll . . .' There was a momentary pause as Gryphon looked around. He felt smaller somehow, smaller than he had felt for years, small and powerless.

'What . . . kill us, Gryphon?' One spoke up sharply. 'You've already done that and can never do it again,' the being concurred. He was smiling. The chamber was getting fuller and fuller as more of the dead arrived. There were all shapes and sizes; every one of them was of the Sand Clan. This was the overwhelming concentration of one clan, one people...the people of Sand City. It was surreal, like watching a silent performance of the world's biggest choir. Gryphon's power was weakening, until eventually, and finally, it drained all together.

'No, no, this can't be happening,' he bellowed. He no longer had control of the situation and a deep-seated horror filled him. Via had regained his old shape and stood once more, this time with all his people around him.

'We are the people of Sand City. We are of the Sand Clan,' they said in unison.

'Stay back, stay back, I am lord here. I am in charge.' He ranted like a child, but his voice depleted to a squeak. He started to fade in much the same way as Via had just done.

His bulbous body became weak and faded and then faded some more until it completely disappeared. There were only the remnants of a faraway echo and, finally, that was gone too! The light dulled to a glow and then extinguished altogether.

'Our work is done here,' the vast collective said in harmony. The boy who had first entered came up alongside Via.

'It's time to go, Uncle,' he said, whilst looking up into Via's eyes. Via looked down with fondness and smiled.

'I'll be along in a moment, Krass,' he said. The boy turned to his parents and Via gave them a nod. Slowly, each and every member of Sand City, their job now complete, returned to their resting place.

Via was now free to join his relatives and friends to cross over. He stepped forward and stood in front of them. Shelley, Katie, Kevin and Monkey were standing together.

'I have to take the Cric with me now,' he said softly.

'But you can't, Via, how can we return to the surface without it to open up the doorway?' Shelley expressed with concern. 'And Katie needs to get home.'

'Don't worry about me, Shelley, I'm staying in Reflections,' she answered.

'There is another path back to the surface. Davenport can lead you there,' Via said. He approached the throne and retrieved the stone. 'I must take this away from all that can harm my people. Take it to a place where no one can find it,' he said and turned to them for the last time. 'Thank you,' he said simply. Once he'd conveyed his message he melted away until only the five of them were left in the chamber. They all looked at each other in silence.

'We must return to the surface,' Shelley said and they all nodded.

'We need him for that.' Kevin said, pointing towards the fallen Davenport. Kevin walked to where his body was strewn and picked up his knife and slipped it back in his trousers. Before anyone could say anything to stop her, Shelley picked up Davenport's rifle and smashed it in half against one of the stone chairs, to the total astonishment of Kevin, but he said nothing.

'We have to wake him,' Katie said with trepidation. 'Come on old man, get up.' She prodded his shoulder and he came to.

'Wha-what's happening?' he snorted.

'It's all over, old man. You've lost your dogs, your weapon and the stone,' Kevin said with relish. 'Now you have to lead us all to the surface or we will all die down here.'

Davenport wasn't going to try anything; there was no point really, he wasn't a threat any more, so he guided them up through the rocks. They walked along and Katie pondered.

'The only thing I don't understand,' Katie said with thought. 'What was Sub Reflections to do with Mad Maisey? I mean it was under her house and the Voice in the Void led us there, but what was it to do with her? Did she actually know about it?'

'I can answer that,' Davenport uttered and everyone looked on in amazement. 'She is my sister!' More looks of shock. 'She showed me the entrance one day, but she never went down below. It must have been where the Sand People first made their way below ground, a quiet place where they thought no one would look.' He continued, 'I went down when she showed me and could only go so far as that rock wall. I found this way down later, but my poor sister lost her mind and forgot all about it.' He said no more.

For the first time since meeting Davenport, they found a softer side to him.

He returned to his old town of Scatterbrook where Shelley and Kevin had first encountered him. He would end his days there.

One of the first things Shelley did when she got back

was to gather the people of Reflections together and tell them the good news. This brought on celebrations for the townsfolk and their new Princess Shelley of Reflections. Afterwards, Shelley, Katie, Kevin and Monkey all shared a dinner together.

'Katie,' Shelley asked, 'what will you do now? In fact you can do whatever you like here,' she said, feeling happy that her best friend would be staying with her for ever.

'I have a new life here in Reflections. I never wanted to go back anyway, Shel.'

'Look Katie, you're my best friend, you know that. We can achieve many things together here. You can help me,' Shelley said, nodding in compliance.

'We have a lot of work to do,' Kevin said in between mouthfuls of potato. 'We have to bring Reflections to its former glory.'

'I'll help as much as I can, too,' Monkey chipped in.

'I'm so lucky to have so many friends surrounding me,' Shelley said with appreciation and smiled fondly. They ate and talked over the plans for the new style Reflections, until Katie spoke up.

'Shelley, I've decided.' She spoke with a determination in her voice. Kevin and Monkey looked on in anticipation.

'What have you decided, Katie? It sounds scary. I don't think I'm going to like this,' Shelley admitted.

'I've decided that I want to explore all of this country.' She sipped her tea as she said it. Shelley just looked at her. 'Who knows what is beyond Reflections? Maybe there are more people out there that need our help. I just want to spend time exploring,' Katie said with a real excitement.

'I'm going, too. Yes, I'm going, too.' Monkey looked into Katie's eyes. 'You can't go without me,' he said abruptly. 'What would you do without me?'

'All right then, we'll both go.' Katie's eyes were bright and excited.

'But what about us?' Kevin chipped in unexpectedly, a look of sheer horror on his face. 'We've just all got back together and now we're going to be split again.'

'Yes, Katie, I'll miss you two terribly, we need your help here,' Shelley said, showing her concern.

'What about you two, you don't need us. Shelley, you've done fine up to now, haven't you? You and Kevin have to run this place and you'll continue to keep it safe for my return. Because when I *do* return, I will stay here for ever. Just let me do this, Shel. I've spent a really bad year without you and everyone here. I need time to relax and chill out. I will come back and we can spend the rest of our lives together.' There was nothing more to say that would change her mind. Shelley could tell, and relented with a sullen look.

'I will miss you like crazy, you know!' she said, as tears welled up in her eyes. 'Let's raise our glasses, then, to running Reflections, and the safe return of Katie and Monkey.' They toasted and laughed and talked until the early hours about their adventures up until this point. The next day, however, when Shelley met Kevin at the breakfast table, there was a note. It simply said: *Until we meet again, all our love, Katie and Monkey . . .*

'Come on, Kevin,' Shelley said as they finished up breakfast. 'We have a job to do.' Kevin smiled; he'd missed that stern determination that he loved so much about Shelley.

'OK Shel, what shall we take on first?' he said, feeling confident in his abilities.

'Well Kev, you're in charge of policing Reflections now. You are the peacekeeper. What do you want to do first?' she said.

'Wow, I had no idea,' he said. 'Thank you, Princess.'

'It's Shelley, Kevin, and always will be. You know that.' Then she laughed.

And so life went on in Reflections under the new rule of Princess Shelley Vendor of Reflections.

Katie and Monkey spent several years roaming the land of Reflections and came across many deadly and strange creatures. They had many adventures of their own before they returned to Shelley and Kevin.

But maybe that is another story . . .